DAMAGED GOODS

A Higher Education Mystery

ANN WASWO

Matador
5 Weir Road
Kibworth Beauchamp
Leicester LE8 0LQ, UK
Tel: (+44) 116 279 2299
Fax: (+44) 116 279 2277
Email: books@troubador.co.uk
Web: www.troubador.co.uk/matador

ISBN 978 1848767 492

British Library Cataloguing in Publication Data.
A catalogue record for this book is available from the British Library.

Typeset in 11pt Minion Pro by Troubador Publishing Ltd, Leicester, UK

Matador is an imprint of Troubador Publishing Ltd

Printed in Great Britain by the MPG Books Group, Bodmin and King's Lynn

'What counts can't be counted!'

CHAPTER ONE

4.50 am on Wednesday, the 8th of July. Akiko Sugiyama winced as she looked at the bedside clock but knew there was no chance of any more sleep. At least the jet lag she suffered after flying to Europe from Tokyo was milder than after the return trip. She stretched her shoulders and legs, revelling as she always did on her travels at occupying such a large bed, stood up and opened the heavy curtains at her bedside. The view transfixed her. Two floors below her the garden of the Warden's Lodgings still lay in darkness, save for a thin shaft of light from a window on the ground floor of the building next door, but the horizon beyond was streaked with shimmering rays of pink and gold. The trees on the main quad of Thaddeus Hall were already bathed in the rays, their upper branches a delicate green. Anxious to go outside, she dressed hurriedly in jeans and t-shirt, combed her shoulder-length black hair and tiptoed down the long staircase to the kitchen. Tom, the Warden's son, turned from the window as she opened the kitchen door.

'Jet lag?' he asked. 'How about some coffee?'

'Yes to both, and thanks,' Akiko answered, 'but it's the sunrise that really got to me.'

'I thought you came to England all the time,' Tom said.

'Always in November, I'm afraid,' Akiko replied. 'That's when our meetings are. And it's so dark most of the time. Umm, good coffee!'

Tom turned back to the window and asked, 'What is it about the sunrise that got to you?'

'It's so… so promising,' Akiko said. 'Soft, moist, but cool. Not like Tokyo at this time of year!'

Tom smiled. 'There's rain forecast for later today, but the morning's going to be fine. I was just going to cycle over to the river bank. Care to join me?'

How like his father's smile, Akiko thought. Indeed, how like his father he was in his overall appearance. The same broad forehead and chiselled features, the same six-foot height. She had recognized him immediately when she had emerged into the arrivals lobby at Heathrow the previous evening, even though she hadn't seen him since he was fourteen or fifteen. That must have been about eight years ago, she mused, on her only other visit to Thaddeus Hall, when she'd come to Exton upon Thames from London to spend the weekend with TH's newly appointed Warden, Sir Christopher Ryan, and Lady Ryan. So Tom must now be in his early twenties, just about the age she had been when she had arrived in Lyon to take up a traineeship at Interpol Headquarters. Christopher Ryan, not yet a sir, had invited all the trainees to a reception at the British Consulate, where he was Consul General. So long ago.

'I'm game,' she answered, 'provided you have a bike for someone my size. As you can see, I'm rather short, just five foot two.'

'No problem,' Tom said. 'We still have my sister's bike. The tyres will need pumping up, but it should suit you fine.'

There was a moment's awkward silence. 'It's so very sad about her,' Akiko said. 'She was such a lovely little girl…'

'And then she got meningitis and died,' Tom broke in.

'My parents split up and my father was left with just his wayward son and his Exton college. Shall we get going?' He stood up and motioned toward the back door.

Akiko thought it best to postpone asking any of the questions that immediately occurred to her and stood up, too. Tom opened the door and led the way to the bike rack on the opposite side of the garden. Except for the light in the window of the adjacent building, there were no signs that anyone else was yet awake. It was now 5.25 am.

Within a few minutes Tom and Akiko were pedalling through the deserted streets of East Exton, and soon they crossed the old iron bridge over the mill stream and followed the tree-lined lane that led down to the River Thames. Already exhilarated by the bike ride – so unlike negotiating the treacherous streets of suburban Tokyo! – Akiko gasped in amazement at the broad expanse that now opened before her. A meadow where a few ponies grazed stretched north and south almost as far as the eye could see, and straight ahead was the river, some forty feet wide at this point. On the other side of it was another meadow and behind that, low hills. Akiko could just make out a church spire some distance back from the opposite shore. Birds swooped down into the long grass near the river's edge and the sun shone almost proudly, as if welcoming them to the new day. They made their way through the gate at the end of the lane and onto the towpath.

'It's magnificent,' Akiko said once she had caught her breath. 'So lush, so much life! But why are we the only people here?'

'Some joggers and dog walkers will start appearing around 6.30,' Tom answered. 'But hardly anyone, except maybe a bird watcher or two, bothers to come here at daybreak in summer. Just too early for them. They'd fall asleep right after dinner and miss all the prime time TV at night.'

'And you come?' Akiko asked.

'Because it's so beautiful,' Tom answered. He smiled at her again. 'Especially the light. I've been trying to capture it in my paintings. That's what drives Dad crazy. I was reading English at Cambridge, but I dropped out after my second year. He wants me to finish my degree and become a diplomat like him, or an accountant. Something respectable, at any rate. Not an artist. And I blame my mother for my sister's death.'

Akiko looked at him quizzically. 'You've just answered most of the questions I was planning to ask you later,' she said at last.

'You came here with me this morning, before it was too late to enjoy the view. I figured I owed you something,' Tom replied, looking out across the river. 'Sorry I was so abrupt back in the kitchen. I should have got over it all by now, I suppose.' He turned toward her. 'Are you going to need my help with the vase?'

'Ah yes, the vase,' Akiko said. 'All your father could tell me when he phoned was that it was Kutani and pretty old. It's true I trained with my father in Kutani techniques, but there are several people here in Exton who are more expert at porcelain repairs than I am. I've been wondering why your father called me.'

'To keep it quiet,' Tom said. 'There'd be talk if it was sent to, say, the University Museum or even to London. You know I helped him collect the pieces? He didn't want anyone on the college staff to be involved. The vase just disappeared from the Senior Common Room late at night – taken away to have some sort of special stand made, he told the Steward. I think there are no more than about thirty fragments of varying sizes, and they now await you in the library at the Lodgings.'

'You mean they await us,' Akiko said and was rewarded with another smile.

They got on their bikes again, cycled downriver along the towpath about half a mile to the University Boathouse near Wallingford and then headed up King's Road and off to the right on the Abingdon Road back to Thaddeus Hall. The Warden was standing at the open refrigerator when they entered the kitchen.

'Ah, there you are! Thank you so much for coming, Akiko,' he said as he embraced her. 'I saw those two coffee mugs and decided Tom must have talked you into one of his early morning outings. I hope it whetted your appetite, because I have just about everything in here for a proper breakfast. How about some melon, smoked salmon, scrambled eggs? Tom can do the scrambling, while I make some toast and some fresh coffee.'

Akiko sat down at the kitchen table and watched the two men, father and son, get to work on breakfast. It was pleasant to be waited on, she thought a bit guiltily, and she devoured everything set before her. 'So good,' she said between mouthfuls. 'I didn't realize how hungry I was.'

'I'm sorry I wasn't here when you got in last night,' Sir Christopher said. 'There was a meeting I just couldn't get out of. And you hardly touched the sandwiches my scout left for you. It's no wonder you're famished. Look, I'm afraid I've got another meeting in half an hour. Tom has everything set up for you in the library. Except the Bunsen burner. That has to stay in the kitchen, I'm afraid. I hate to rush you, but TKA4 – that's Thaddeus K. Arkwright IV, our founding benefactor's son – arrives for his annual visit in the middle of next week.'

'No problem,' Akiko replied. 'You made it clear this was urgent when you phoned me the other day, and there's some business I can take care of in Paris while I'm over here. He gave you the vase?'

'Yes, just last July. He said it was from his father's Japanese art collection, and his father had always been meaning to give it to us. Let's see, my secretary has finally unearthed the details that came with it.' Sir Christopher reached into his jacket pocket and withdrew a slip of paper. 'Old Kutani-style vase from the Yoshidaya kilns, c. 1830. Gracefully rounded sides, 52 cm in height. Wide band of yellow enamel top and bottom, a swirl of pale purple enamel peonies with deep green leaves on the white underglaze all around the centre, three blue and yellow butterflies hovering here and there above the flowers. Lightly crackled finish due to age.'

'That sounds quite interesting,' Akiko said after a slight pause, raising her coffee cup for a final swallow. 'How did it get damaged?'

Sir Christopher stiffened. He was silent for a moment and then he answered in a studiously calm voice. 'It was a fight, a fight in the Senior Common Room. Two of the most senior fellows got into a heated argument and one of them started waving his stick at the other. The other grabbed it, and they both crashed into the bookcase where the vase was on display. The vase came flying out and hit a nearby table. They were both just a bit bruised, but the vase was shattered.'

His face was drawn as he continued. 'I was on the other side of the room, so I didn't hear how the argument began.

But it has to have been about the appraisal proposal. It's tearing the fellowship apart.'

'What sort of appraisal?' Akiko asked.

'A damned foolish sort!' Sir Christopher replied with some vehemence. 'A one-size-fits-all model for assessing the research that academics publish no matter what their academic fields. I don't deny the need for accountability, but what started off sensibly enough back in the late 80s has got way out of hand. This latest proposal we were landed with in May...' He glanced at his watch. 'I'm afraid I've got to head off to my meeting in minutes. Shall we take a quick look at the remains of our vase? You'll meet most of the fellows later this week, and I can guarantee you that you'll hear a lot more about appraisal.'

Akiko followed Sir Christopher and Tom to the library. Everything she'd asked for was there: a canvas cloth on the carpet by the window, another cloth on the large desk, two Anglepoise lamps, a tin of epoxy glue, a plastic washing-up bowl and a bag of horticultural sand. Her kit bag filled with tools and a precious supply of lacquer resin and enamel pigments sat by the door, where Tom had left it the night before. Akiko went immediately to the cardboard box on the desk and removed the lid. It didn't take her long to find what she was looking for: the thick round base of the vase, still intact. She turned it over and smiled.

'My great uncle painted this. Look, here's his mark, just here within this rectangle. Back in the 1950s and 60s he was one of the best copyists of the Old Kutani designs that Yoshidaya had revived, but like all of them he put his own mark on his work so there'd be no doubt it was a copy. They used a special firing process to produce the "crackled" finish.

7

There's hardly any early 19th-century Yoshidaya left today, even in Japan; just a few pieces in museums. And most of those are far smaller than this one. I'd say this was definitely made for the export market.'

'So it's a fake?' Sir Christopher stammered, his face flushed.

'Better to think of it as a copy,' Akiko replied calmly, 'and a rather fine copy at that. It's part of the Japanese art tradition, you know, to reproduce old designs, and Kutani porcelain painters, most of them anyway, have been doing just that for the past 100 years or so. Your Mr TKA3 probably paid a lot more than this piece is worth, but it's still worth maybe £4,000 or so. And it will be easier to repair! I know a few tricks for getting close to the Old Kutani colours, but with modern pigments it will be a cinch.'

'It's just as likely that TKA4 found out it was a copy and decided to offload it on us,' Sir Christopher grumbled. 'He's a lot more slippery than his father ever was, and a lot more hands on about his financial support of the College. Just my luck to end up as head of a recent foundation instead of an ancient one with lots of assets from long-dead donors.' He looked at his watch. 'Got to dash, I'm afraid. I've asked the Chef to send us something for an early dinner here in the Lodgings, say about 6.30? There's plenty for lunch in the fridge. Tom will be at your beck and call.'

With that, the Warden left the library, and Tom moved toward the desk. 'What's next?' he asked.

Akiko smiled up at him and said, 'Let me have a look at your hands, please. Fingernails, too.'

There's hardly any early 19th-century Yoshidaya left today, even in Japan; just a few pieces in museums. And most of those are far smaller than this one. I'd say this was definitely made for the export market.'

CHAPTER TWO

Akiko was kneeling at the edge of the canvas by the window and had just lined up the last of the five fragments that made up the top of the vase when she first heard the sirens. She glanced at the clock on the mantle: almost 4.00 pm. She stood up slowly and stretched as Tom came in with their tea.

'Oh I'm so stiff!' she exclaimed. 'All this kneeling was a lot easier when I was your age, I can assure you.'

Then they both turned toward the window. The sirens had grown shrill, and first an ambulance and then a police car turned into the narrow lane at the bottom of which the Lodgings stood. They moved to the window, carefully avoiding the canvas and their painstaking handiwork.

'It's right next door!' Tom exclaimed. 'That's where some of the fellows have their workrooms. Uh-oh, here comes my father, and the Bursar. There must have been an accident of some sort.'

'Then there would just be an ambulance,' Akiko observed. 'This looks a bit more serious, don't you think? Look, there's another car. No uniforms on the men getting out but definitely police, I'd say.' Tom started to turn around, but Akiko put a restraining hand on his arm. 'There's nothing you can do,' she said, 'and you'd only be sent away. We're better off watching from here.'

Just then the Warden looked up at the window and saw

them. As he was about to move in their direction he was intercepted by one of the police constables and led away into the workroom building.

It was a good two hours later when Sir Christopher finally entered the Lodgings. The police had left about half an hour earlier, and the ambulance was just turning the corner at the top of the lane. Akiko poured a large glass of whisky and took it to him in the living room, where he sat crumpled in a leather armchair. 'This might help,' she said simply and sat down in the chair opposite. Tom stood nearby.

'Bates is dead,' Sir Christopher said wearily. 'His research assistant found his body a little after 3.30. The police don't think it was a natural death.' He took a few sips of whisky. 'They've taken away his computer and some of his notebooks. And his body just now, for a post-mortem. Christ, he was almost as old as I am! He'd had serious heart trouble for years. Why couldn't he just have died of heart failure like most of us old men do and let us off with the usual memorial service? "Theodore Bates, distinguished Professor of Medieval History, died as he lived, at his desk in College working on his latest book." I hate to think what the fall-out from this is going to be, however it turns out.'

'What makes the police suspect unnatural causes?' Tom asked.

Sir Christopher took another sip of whisky. 'He left a note. I verified that it was in his handwriting – it took me years to learn how to decipher his scrawl. "Something is wrong, very wrong. Why is this happening? There is only one answer." Pretty vague, isn't it? But that Detective Chief Inspector, Baxter I think his name is, he finds it "worth exploring further".'

'Where was Professor Bates's room?' Akiko asked.

'His room? Why, it's on the ground floor of the building right next door, extending a bit beyond our kitchen. He had a better view from his bow window of the rosery at the edge of my garden than I did. That said, he did bring me some interesting old varieties from his garden over the years.'

'So it was his room where the light was on at dawn this morning. I noticed it when I opened my curtains. Didn't you notice it, too?' Akiko asked, looking at Tom. 'Every other window except the kitchen window here and the ground floor window next door was dark when we went out.'

'That's not possible,' Sir Christopher said before Tom could answer. 'Bates was away at a conference in York and didn't get back to Exton until early this afternoon. He was almost too late for lunch. I saw him when he rushed into the Fellows' Dining Room a little after 1.30 and spoke to him briefly in the SCR later.'

'The scouts don't arrive until 6.30 in the morning,' Tom interjected. 'I see them going in to clean when I get back from the river. We left at least an hour before then.'

'So why was the light on?' asked Akiko.

Sir Christopher stood up a bit unsteadily. 'I'm not sure I want to know,' he muttered, 'but I've just heard the back door close, which means our supper has arrived. We could all use some nourishment, couldn't we? And let's talk about something else for a bit. DCI Baxter is due to drop by later this evening, and I could use a break.'

They filed into the dining room and found heaping platters of roast chicken, assorted salads, cheese and fruit being laid out on the buffet by one of the Hall scouts. 'Thanks, Mary, and give my thanks to the Chef,' Sir Christopher said. 'Akiko, do help yourself while I open some wine.' Soon all three were seated at the large dining table, eyes downcast, nibbling at their food.

Akiko broke the silence after several minutes. 'It's the same everywhere, isn't it? Tell people they can't talk about something, and it's all they can think of talking about,' she observed, looking hopefully in Tom's direction.

'What we need,' Tom responded gamely, 'is some music to distract us.' He went to the shelf of CDs in the living room across the entry hall and ruffled through the disks. 'Ah, here we are. Mozart's *Divertimento in D Major…*'

Sir Christopher chuckled, and he visibly relaxed as the lyrical music flowed into the dining room. 'So how was your day with our vase?' he asked Akiko as they were helping themselves to cheese and fruit.

'A bit better than I expected,' she replied. 'There's less damage to the top and bottom than to the middle. It must have been the middle that hit the edge of the table, and the white background there will help mask the repairs. Thanks to Tom's help, I've got all the fragments laid out, and I'm pretty sure I can make the whole thing look presentable. Especially if you put it in a proper display case, so no one, especially not TKA4, can pick it up and examine it closely.'

'Good idea,' Sir Christopher replied. 'Obviously that's what we should have done in the first place, but who was to know the SCR was about to become a battleground? Tom! More diverting music, please. The real world is coming back! And could you make us some coffee?'

Tom slipped another disk into the CD player, this time of Strauss waltzes. He'd just delivered the coffee and noted approvingly that his father and Akiko were talking and laughing on their side of the table when the doorbell rang. Everyone froze.

Sir Christopher got up resignedly and went to the front door. 'Do come in, Inspector,' he said. 'This way, please, and I'll introduce you to my house guest and son. They may have some information that will be of use to you.'

DCI James Baxter stepped inside, followed by a younger man. 'This is Detective Constable Sanderson,' he said. 'He'll take notes, as needed. Sorry to interrupt your supper – and the music. It's the best cure for a bad day, isn't it?'

'Indeed,' replied Sir Christopher, relieved he wasn't suspected of celebrating the demise of one of his fellows. 'And this is Ms Akiko Sugiyama, the Director of Art Watch East in Tokyo, who is visiting us for a few days. And my son, Tom.'

'Art Watch East, is it? We've done some work in common with Interpol, haven't we?' Baxter said as he shook Akiko's hand. 'It's a pleasure to meet you at long last. And you, too, Tom.'

Tom shook the DCI's hand and turned to the constable. 'Hi, Sandy. Somebody told me you'd joined the Thames Valley force.'

'Hi, Ryan,' Sanderson replied. 'I heard you were back in Exton.'

'So you two know each other,' Baxter stated matter-of-factly. 'Everybody in Exton under the age of twenty-five seems to know everyone else. Well, how about if I give you some time to reminisce later, after we finish with our current enquiry? Warden, you said Ms Sugiyama and Tom might have some useful information?'

'There was a light on in Professor Bates's room at dawn

this morning,' Akiko said. 'I saw it clearly from my bedroom window when I opened the curtains a little after 4.50. I woke up that early because of jet lag, having just arrived from Tokyo last night. The light was still on when Tom and I left for the river about half an hour later. Of course, I didn't know it was his window at the time. It was the ground floor window in the building just next door, down and to the left from my window on the second floor of the Lodgings. My room is way up above the kitchen, facing southeast, judging from the sunrise.'

'Eminently clear, Ms Sugiyama. I can tell you're a professional. You got that down, Sanderson? You confirm that, Tom?' Baxter looked over at Tom, who nodded affirmatively. 'Right then, we'll check that out. Now would you two excuse us? I've got a few questions for the Warden.'

Akiko and Tom retreated to the kitchen, closing the door behind them. 'Whew,' said Tom, 'Baxter certainly doesn't waste any time on niceties.'

'Down-to-Basics Baxter, I think that's what my contact at Interpol called him,' Akiko replied, yawning. 'But it did end up saving a lot of time on the case, not to mention saving money on faxes! He has a nicer voice than I'd imagined.'

'How did you get into fighting art crime anyway?' Tom asked.

Akiko looked at him thoughtfully for a moment. 'It was a way to escape from home, from my father. I was an only child, and as a daughter I was expected not only to learn the family craft, but also to marry a talented young painter who would carry on the family name. I did all that, but when my husband died in a motorcycle accident less than a year after our marriage, I reflected on my situation. There I was, barely twenty-one, out in a lovely but remote village in Ishikawa prefecture. I knew I was a pretty mediocre painter – my eye was always better than my hand. I wasn't good enough to be part of the movement to take Kutani forward, as a few of my friends have done. And, well, I was getting bored with reproducing all those old designs, wonderful though they are.'

Akiko took a long drink of water before continuing. 'So I talked my father into adopting one of my late husband's younger brothers as his son, and I joined the Tokyo Police as a "junior art assistant". That was in 1980, when thefts of valuable antiques from isolated houses in the Japanese countryside were just beginning to escalate, and they needed someone who could take down the details accurately. A year or so later I got an Interpol traineeship in France to learn about the illicit international trade in cultural properties and antiques. The "bubble economy" was booming when I got back to Tokyo, and there were an awful lot of art transactions taking place, some of them pretty dodgy. The little "art section" in Police HQ was swamped with work, more and more of it having to do with imported items, so Art Watch East was set up as a semi-independent operation. I was appointed director of it about six years ago. My organization is basically a clearing house for information. We help others "fight art crime", as you put it. Every once in a while, though, we do get a bit more directly involved.'

'What does your father think of what you're doing now?' Tom asked.

'We didn't see that much of each other after I left, I'm afraid,' Akiko replied. 'But I stayed with him during his last days, not long ago, and he showed me a scrapbook he had kept of newspaper clippings about me and Art Watch East. He said he was pleased he had let me leave home.'

There was a long silence. Then Akiko said, 'I have got to go to bed now. But will you show me some of your paintings tomorrow? There'll be time while the glue is drying.'

'Yes, I'd be very happy to do that,' Tom replied.

Akiko slipped out the side door of the kitchen, glanced at the closed doors to the living room, from behind which muffled voices were audible, and headed wearily upstairs.

CHAPTER THREE

Baxter and Sanderson emerged from the Lodgings about 8.30 pm. 'They're all alike, these heads of Exton colleges,' Baxter grumbled as he thrust himself into the driver's seat of his car and headed off toward Abingdon. 'They stress how willing they are to help with our enquiries, and then they remain as evasive as the worst criminals I've ever encountered. Did you notice how the Warden reacted when I asked him if there'd been anything unusual about Bates's behaviour in recent weeks?'

'Well, sir, maybe he looked a bit pensive?' Sanderson ventured.

'Pensive, my foot! Calculating is more like it,' Baxter retorted. 'Figuring out how little he could get away with telling me, I'd say. I read the papers, and I play tennis with a couple of Exton dons who are about my age. I know how many tensions all these reform initiatives have created within the University over recent years, and I don't believe Thaddeus Hall has managed to escape them. Bates may have been "undoubtedly one of the most distinguished medieval historians in Europe", as the Warden put it, and "eagerly awaiting publication of the book he had just completed", but he can't have been immune to all the changes that have been proposed in how universities, including this one, should operate in future. Nor can any of the others, the Warden included. Now, tell me what you came up with this afternoon.'

'Yes, sir,' Sanderson replied, relieved to be back on the factual ground he felt most comfortable with. He opened his notebook and turned it toward the car window to catch the lingering mid-summer twilight. 'Well, as you probably know, sir, Thaddeus Hall is one of the seven graduate colleges in Exton and like most of the others it was founded in the 1960s. We have a complete list of fellows and staff from the Bursar, and we know the names of the seventeen fellows who have workrooms in the same building as the deceased. Nine have been out of the country since at least mid-June. One of them is in Timbuktu, of all places! The Bursar is arranging interviews for us with the other eight for tomorrow morning, starting at 10.00, in a room near his office in the Old School Building, and he is willing to arrange other meetings with other fellows as and when we wish. And PC Giles will be interviewing all the scouts who have anything to do with that building when they come off shift tomorrow. Professor Bates himself was a lifelong bachelor, but we're getting in touch with some of his relatives up north. Giles should have finished checking out his house in North Exton by now.

'I got a map of Thaddeus Hall from the Head Porter. A high stone wall encircles about two-thirds of the site – the original Old School grounds that TH took over, along with the Old School Building itself. The northern boundary wall was removed when they built the Fellows' Building and dining hall before opening up for business. There are only low boundary walls, with hedges and the like behind them, from the Warden's Lodgings, the other old building on the site, then up School Lane past the Fellows' Building and around the corner to the Hall, but the security on all of those buildings – doors and ground floor windows – is pretty good, and there are high wrought-iron fences set some way back between the buildings. There are two entries to the Fellows' Building from the Lane, but both have had decent access systems since the late 1990s: swipe-cards for occupants and room-specific buzzers for visitors – and the doors lock automatically after any entry.

'It turns out the single back door to this building, from within TH itself, is open most of the day every day, but there are coded gates at all access points to the main grounds. Same code for all gates, the Head Porter said, and the code hasn't been changed in years, but still it's unlikely that any outsider could have got into the building last night or early this morning. If someone had, getting into Bates's room would most likely have been a doddle, because he was notorious for forgetting to lock his office door. Apparently he kept the key under a pot plant on a nearby windowsill. The door was unlocked when his research assistant arrived for their regular weekly appointment this afternoon. We found the key in Bates's pocket.

'One other thing, sir. The window in his room that faces the Lodgings is high up, maybe five feet above floor level, with a wall-to-wall bookshelf underneath. He had some files and other stuff piled up on top of most of the bookshelf, and the curtain was pulled to one side to make room for them. So even though the curtains on the bow window, the one facing onto the main quad, had been closed, the shaft of light that Japanese woman saw would have been visible nearby.'

'Get a list of Bates's graduate students, too,' Baxter said, 'and set up interviews with them. You handle those. And learn how to pronounce the name of "that Japanese woman":

ah-key-co sue-gi-yah-mah. That's "gi" as in gift. If we ever have another case like the one in the Cotswolds a few years ago, we're likely to need her again. She knows what's going on in East Asian art markets, legally or otherwise. More attractive than I'd imagined, too.'

He turned into the driveway of Abingdon Police Station and parked near the entry door. 'You can head home for the night, Sandy. I'm just going to see if there are any messages for me. I'll meet you back here at 9.15 tomorrow morning. It's the summer vacation, so the traffic won't be as bad as usual. We should have no trouble getting to Thaddeus Hall well before 10.00.' With that, Baxter headed up the entry steps and down the long corridor to his office.

As he had hoped, there was a memo from their IT technician on his desk: 'Have taken a quick look at the Bates computer. Nothing out of the ordinary so far on the hard drive, except for the email. Both the inbox and sent mail folders had been deleted on the morning of 6 July. EUCS will forward us the restored records tomorrow morning, and we'll have print-outs ready for you by midday. The unit attached to the computer is for medical monitoring. I'm in touch with the NHS about it.'

Baxter chuckled. 'You can delete, but you cannot hide,' he murmured to himself, grateful that so few academics and students within the University were yet aware that its computing service automatically recorded all email folders on its network every night and kept the tapes for at least a month. Under strict 'lock and key', of course, but the relevant authorities could get at them, as could careless users who had deleted their own folders by mistake. The retrieved folders had proven useful in sorting out any number of local crimes and misdemeanours in the past, and might well be helpful in this case, too, he reckoned, since Bates seemed pretty computer-savvy for a medievalist. 'A leading role in the digitalisation of 12th – and 13th – century records,' the Warden had said, 'and in constant contact with researchers around the world.'

He had just switched off the lights in his office and swung his jacket over his shoulder when his mobile rang. It was the Warden.

'I'm sorry to be phoning so late,' Sir Christopher said, 'but I thought you should know that Bates left the conference in York late yesterday afternoon, not this morning as I had thought. The organizer, Dr Thompson, called me just a few minutes ago to find out if Bates was all right. Apparently he had said he was feeling unwell. Thompson had become alarmed when he got no answer at Bates's home either this morning or this evening, and finally he phoned me. Naturally, he was distraught at the news.'

'Yes, of course,' Baxter replied, genuinely surprised that the Warden was volunteering information that might prove awkward for his college. 'Many thanks for letting me know. I'll be in touch with you again tomorrow, after we've completed our interviews.'

CHAPTER 4

The Bursar's secretary tapped lightly on the door of the temporary interview room in the Old School Building before opening it and quickly stepping inside. 'I'm terribly sorry,' she said, 'but the Bursar has just had a call from Professor Avery-Hill. He's at BBC Exton now about to record an interview for "The World at One" and won't be able to make his appointment at noon. He wonders if he could see you after 2.00 but before 3.30 when he has an important meeting? The Bursar would be happy to offer you lunch at 12.45 if you care to stay on.'

Baxter glanced at his watch and, with effort, suppressed a frown. It was just 11.55, and Avery-Hill was to have been the last of the eight fellows he and Sanderson were seeing that morning. 'Please thank the Bursar for his invitation,' he said in as neutral a tone as he could muster, 'but I think I'll head back to my office. Please ask the Bursar to tell the Professor I'll see him here at 2.30, and do ask the Bursar to remind him that this is a police enquiry, with which his cooperation would be much appreciated.'

'Yes, sir, I will do that,' the secretary said as she backed out of the doorway and closed the door.

Baxter turned to Sanderson and let his frown come forth. 'So some event somewhere far away is more important than a mysterious death here in Exton yet again. I've heard this

Avery-Hill chap on the BBC before and seen him on "Newsnight" a few times. Some sort of expert on international conflict resolution, not that he and his ilk have yet managed to make the world a safer place with all their theories. Okay, let's head back to Abingdon.'

'Uh, I'm having lunch with Tom Ryan,' Sanderson said. 'He...'

Baxter looked at him sternly. 'I thought I told you to postpone your reminiscences until after this enquiry was over.'

'It's not that, sir,' Sanderson stammered. 'Tom left a message at the station for me late last night, saying he'd just met up with some students in the college bar and they were mightily upset at the news of Bates's death. He thought it might be a good idea if he took me to lunch with a few of them, to sort of get a sense of their concerns in an informal setting. We're all about the same age, after all.'

Baxter nodded appreciatively. 'Good idea on his part, and smart of you to take him up on it. I'll meet you back here at 2.15 to hear a bit more about those concerns.'

On the drive back to Abingdon Baxter reflected on the morning's interviews. Seven college fellows, three in the humanities and four in the social sciences. Curious there were no engineers or scientists with workrooms in the Fellows' Building. Some sort of segregation? He must ask the Warden about that. And the three women he'd interviewed – a lecturer in Islamic art and architecture, a geographer and a sociologist – all had adjacent rooms on the upper floor. Maybe that was only so they could lay claim to the lavatory at their end of the inner workroom corridor, but he'd ask about that, too. It was certainly the case that the women had been fond of Bates and were visibly upset by his death. More so than the four men, perhaps, although the lecturer in modern British history and the professor of English literature had both said, what was it? Ah yes: 'Such a loss to the cause.' He'd asked them what cause they were referring to, of course, although he'd had a pretty good idea it had something to do with university reform, and he'd been a bit surprised by the specificity of their replies. 'The book,' the historian had said. 'Bates was one of its most eloquent defenders, and we'll probably lose the battle to preserve it now that he's gone.' The professor had echoed his younger colleague's pessimism: 'Without Bates, the academic book is doomed. It's going to be articles only from now on. Metrics will prevail.' Baxter wished Sanderson were with him in the car so he could have him read out his notes on metrics and get a firmer grip on precisely what they were. After lunch he'd do just that.

None of the seven had seen Bates since Monday morning, when he'd stopped by his workroom briefly on his way to catch the train to York, and lunchtime on Wednesday. None had been in the Fellows' Building after about 8.00 pm on Tuesday night and, not surprisingly, none had been there at dawn on Wednesday. Nor could any of them shed any useful light on Bates's note. 'Any of us could have written that,' was how the politics lecturer had put it, 'except only a medievalist would think there was a single answer to the problems we're facing these days.' The sociologist, Dr Adele Williamson, had chatted with Bates over coffee after lunch on Wednesday and walked back to the Fellows' Building with him at about 2.15. 'Such a kindly man, always so supportive of the younger fellows like me,' she'd said, dabbing at her eyes with a crumpled tissue. 'Just as we were going our separate ways he wished me well on my research trip to Guatemala later this month. I guess I was probably the last person to see him alive.' She gratefully received the fresh tissue Sanderson handed her at that point.

Baxter got himself a sandwich and a soft drink at the staff canteen and made his way to his office. There was a message from the Chief Pathologist on his answering machine, asking him to call her back. Baxter pressed the mortuary button on his phone straight away, hoping to catch her before her lunch break.

'Louise? James here. You have something for me?'

'Yes indeed,' Louise Mason replied, quickly swallowing the bite of sandwich she had just taken at her office desk. 'No doubt about the cause of Bates's death. A massive myocardial infarction. I've spoken to his consultant here at the hospital, and he said he is sad but not surprised by the news. Bates had his first heart attack about six years ago, and he hadn't been the best of patients thereafter: still long hours at work, lots of good food and drink. There are a couple of surprising findings, though. He was on warfarin, of course, but there were no traces of warfarin in his system post-mortem. And he had one of those new-fangled INR monitoring devices attached to his computer so he could self-test the clotting tendencies of his blood at regular intervals and adjust his meds if necessary. But the consultant says the ID number I gave him, which I got from your IT technician, is not the number of the device he issued to Bates. He's checking with his registrar now to see whose device it might have been. Apparently there are at least fifteen of them in use in Exton colleges at the moment. As you know, there's a private health insurance plan available as a fringe benefit to college fellows, and those who opt for it can get some forms of medical care long before they'd get it on the NHS.'

'Someone else's device, you say?' Baxter exclaimed. 'And we know Bates was always leaving his door unlocked! This might explain his note. He finally figured out that "something was wrong" with what the device was telling him to do, but by then it was too late. A hi-tech medical device as murder weapon. Now that would be a first.'

'Steady on, James,' Louise counselled. 'So far as I'm aware these devices just give objective readings from a tiny pinprick of blood onto a special pad, and the user records the results on a standard onscreen chart and follows instructions to increase or decrease his meds if necessary to get back into the recommended range. There's not much room for foul play there. And there's another possibility, too: that Bates simply stopped taking the warfarin all on his own, just because he was tired of life and ready to die. It wouldn't be the first time that had happened. At any rate, I need a bit more info before I sign off on him.'

'I appreciate that,' Baxter said. 'Thanks for reminding me of the other possibility, and do keep me posted about whatever you discover, old girl. I'm going to be over at Thaddeus Hall most of the afternoon, but I'll be checking my messages on my mobile and back here later this evening.'

'You will be checking for messages all night, if I know you, James,' Louise said wearily, 'but I'm off duty at 6.00 and if you haven't heard from me by then, don't expect anything until tomorrow. Some of us have a life beyond work, you know, and I'm going out to dinner with friends this evening. Have you been out to dinner with friends in living memory?'

'Point taken,' Baxter responded. 'Okay if I call you someday for help with my first time in ages? No need to answer that. I hope your sandwich today is tastier than mine. Bye for now.'

Baxter put the receiver down gently and started shuffling through the stack of files on his desk. It didn't take him long to find the file of recovered emails from Bates's computer. He leaned back in his desk chair, sandwich in one hand and print-outs in the other. There were a lot of messages between Bates and Avery-Hill interspersed among those between Bates and his students and fellow medievalists around the world. Baxter decided to concentrate on the former for the time being and after a few minutes' reading he decided he might well have a very interesting interview ahead of him at 2.30. He swallowed the last bite of his sandwich and began reading in earnest.

* * *

Meanwhile, Akiko had met the Warden at 12.45 at his office, and together they had headed off across the lawn to Hall, served themselves from the buffet and taken seats in the Fellows' Dining Room. Sir Christopher introduced her to the two fellows seated opposite as 'an old friend who has had the misfortune of visiting us at a difficult time' and looked expectantly at his colleagues. Dr Owen Magnusson, an economist, was the first to respond.

'Truly sad about Bates,' he said in a suitably muted tone of voice. 'But everyone is wondering why the police were called in. Surely it was just an old man – a very nice old man, to be sure – having his last heart attack?'

'You may very well be right,' Sir Christopher replied, and he then explained about the note Bates had left. 'The police have to check such things out, but I'm fairly sure they'll be satisfied there's nothing more to it, and life will get back to normal soon.'

'Normal?' interjected Dr Raymond Chang, a specialist in modern Chinese literature. 'Life will never get back to normal here, and without Bates it's likely to get worse.'

'Now really, Ray', said Magnusson. 'You know you're on the losing side, and you'd have lost even if you still had Bates to bat for you. These changes are the only sensible way forward. Once they're in place, HEFCE will leave us alone for decades.'

'Excuse me,' said Akiko, 'but what is this heff-ke?'

'It's the acronym for the Higher Education Funding Council for England,' said Sir Christopher, leaning in her direction. 'It provides block grants of public money to universities for teaching and research. Even Exton, which has significant financial resources of its own, depends on those block grants for a substantial portion of its basic operating costs every year.' Then, looking back across the table at his colleagues, he added, 'It's what HEFCE asks for in return, either directly or indirectly through other bodies, that bothers some academics.'

'Because they take it too seriously,' Magnusson retorted. 'HEFCE just wants to make universities more accountable for the public funding they receive and more efficient in their governance. Provided we let our administration play the game and file all the reports they ask for, we academics can go about our teaching and research pretty much as usual.'

'Not so!' Chang exclaimed. 'In the last research assessment exercise, I was excluded because none of my publications – three translations of Chinese novels and a book on 19th-century Chinese literature – could be counted as "research". The translations were "just a mechanical exercise" and the book, "just a survey". All that counts as "research" these days is what scientists do in their labs or what people like you, Owen, do with the latest economic data. And then it had better be published in an academic journal that is also available online so that the number of citations it receives in that and other journals can be tallied up at the push of a button.'

'But you see, Ray,' Magnusson said, 'that's where the future of scholarship lies. We Exton economists gave up writing books years ago, and we all know that students don't want to buy, much less read, books these days. They're tuned in to the Internet, and they want articles, preferably available online so they can read them in the comfort of their own rooms. And so do our colleagues throughout the world. They don't have the time to read books anymore, and libraries don't have the money to buy many of them, given the high cost of databases and e-resources. You people in the humanities are not just writing about the past, you're trying to live in it. But times have changed. Why, you would have had no trouble getting into the last assessment exercise if you had simply published four chapters of your book as articles first.'

Chang stared at him angrily. 'My book is a coherent whole,' he muttered. 'The analysis is cumulative. There are issues and themes that demand extended exploration, not a few 12-page articles.'

Sir Christopher rose to his feet slowly and suggested they continue the conversation over coffee in the SCR. Both Chang and Magnusson begged off, saying they had to get back to their workrooms, so the Warden and Akiko headed downstairs alone.

'I see what you mean about tension,' Akiko said as they reached the bottom of the stairs.

'That's not the half of it,' Sir Christopher muttered as he ushered her into the SCR and poured them each a cup of coffee. As soon as they were seated in a quiet corner he said, 'What's adding to the tension now is a proposal from our central administration for a supposedly "fair and efficient" appraisal system for all the holders of academic posts to monitor their contributions to research activity within the University. A simple one-page form for everyone to fill out just once a year in place of the deluge of forms and questionnaires they've received over the past two decades. They list their publications for the year, their ongoing research projects, the number of graduate students they supervise and their pro rata share of the external funding that the research cluster they belong to has received. There's a section on "public engagement", too, including media exposure and contacts with research "users" in business and other national or international organizations.'

'And the problem with that?' Akiko asked.

'Both in the assumptions behind the questions asked and the uses to which the answers are going to be put,' Sir Christopher replied glumly. 'In the proposed plan publishing a book counts for no more than publishing an article, so long as the article is published in a "high-ranking" journal, however that may be determined. A book targeted at an audience beyond academe might just do better than an article, but only if sales figures – or income received from the sale of film or TV rights – are above a certain level. A co-authored publication of either sort, especially when one of the co-authors is a graduate student or a post-doctoral fellow, gets more points than a sole-authored work.'

'Why does co-authorship, especially with a graduate student or post-doc, count for more than sole-authorship?' Akiko asked.

'Good question,' Sir Christopher replied. 'It's seen as part of the "capacity-building" role of senior academics, bringing younger scholars along, and besides it's what they've been doing in the sciences for years. "The more minds to the task, the better the outcome" and, one might add, the more articles possible from a single project. The solo scholar is a bit suspect these days: thought to be insufficiently engaged with wider discourses beyond academe and more concerned with putting his or her own stamp on the field than in making "useful" contributions to knowledge. It's okay to write a book or two on your own toward the end of your academic career, once you've earned your stripes, but essential to work with others earlier on to make sure your efforts contribute to the achievement of government objectives for proper "knowledge transfer" and "beneficial outcomes" for the UK. Making everyone part of a research cluster is designed, in large part, to discourage "useless" research that is driven merely by an individual scholar's curiosity and to encourage research that seems to satisfy national needs.'

Sir Christopher took a final sip of coffee and stared out the SCR window. 'Then there's the real sting in the tail,' he said quietly. 'Thus far the impact of assessment has been collective, based on external peer review and determining the block grants that universities receive from the state and then devolve, according to composite scores earned, to their faculties. This scheme is in addition to that, and it's going to impact on the individual post-holder. Some fancy algorithms will be applied to the annual reports and overall scores determined. Those with low scores will be "invited to consultations about their career development". Those with average scores will receive modest bonuses for the year. Those with high scores will receive substantial bonuses, and if they get high scores in three of the following four years they'll qualify for promotion to higher ranks and a permanent increase in their salaries. Quite a change in both ethos and practice and it's got the humanities scholars particularly alarmed. Like Ray Chang, whom you met at lunch today. Not to mention a few social scientists who still like to tackle big subjects in books, or even small subjects which they can then examine in detail. Not surprisingly, it usually takes rather longer to write a book than an article, so these people are particularly upset. As I mentioned to you yesterday, it's a one-size-fits-all proposal – easier to manage that way, I suppose, and the managers within the University now hold sway.'

Just then a heavyset man in a rumpled tweed jacket entered the now almost-vacant SCR. 'Ah, there's Elliot Jameson, our Management Studies don,' Sir Christopher said as he stood up. 'Elliot! Do come join us,' he called out warmly, adding in a much lower tone of voice, 'I've just been attempting to explain the new appraisal scheme to my visitor, but I'm sure you can explain the background to it all better than I can.'

Jameson gave a world-weary smile as he shook Akiko's hand. 'My wife is Music Fellow at St Julian's, so the Warden thinks I have balanced views. I'm not so sure about that, but I'll give it a try.' He settled into an adjacent chair and cleared his throat. 'The way I see it,' he said, 'we're now at stage 3 of a process that began several decades ago with efforts to reform the National Health Service. Back in the 1970s our hospitals were providing good care, "free at the point of need" to patients in keeping with the founding principles of the NHS,' he observed, 'but more money from the state was required every year in order to do so. And it turned out the doctors didn't know how much any of the procedures they were carrying out cost. A hip replacement, say, or cancer treatment. They just did the work they deemed necessary, and if their hospital overspent its budget they figured that was someone else's problem. Well, when the Tories came to power under Mrs Thatcher in 1979, intent on cutting taxes and controlling public expenditure, they didn't like that situation at all. Assaulting the NHS was risky politically, but by the late 1980s they had installed what they considered a proper "management tier" in hospitals and in the NHS as a whole. Instead of clerks who just paid the bills as they came in, there were now experts in cost analysis, resource allocation, time management and the like. And a host of new terms – mission statements, benchmarks, transparency, stakeholders – also borrowed from the corporate world and its regulators. Hospitals, and the NHS as a whole, were to become more "business-like", so that taxpayers got the most from their "investments", just like in the corporate sector.'

Jameson took a sip of coffee and continued. 'Well, similar policies were applied at roughly the same time to other parts of the public sector, including universities, all but one of which in this country are publicly funded. I gather that's not the case in your country, Ms Sugiyama, and also not in the USA. But it is the case here and in most of continental Europe. So we, too, soon got our marching orders from the

Conservatives to become more "business-like" and "responsive to national manpower needs", and that pressure continued under New Labour after 1997, along with demands to admit more students and, more recently, to focus on what is described as "economically and socially useful" research.

'From a management studies point of view, not to mention the changing demographics that made all governments in the developed world concerned about escalating public spending, some of these policy initiatives made more than a bit of sense. Like hospitals, universities didn't really know what their diverse activities were costing either, and the tab just kept growing year on year. There were some pretty primitive accounting methods in operation, too, especially in ancient universities like this one.

'But,' Jameson said with emphasis, as he noticed that the Warden was getting a bit restive, 'there was a major difference between government policy toward the NHS and the universities. The public admired doctors of medicine, and thus so too must politicians. Those doctors were fine at doctoring, they were just lousy administrators. Get some proper management experts into the NHS and all would be well. Whether that's the case or not is controversial, but I won't go into that. The point is that academics didn't have such a good public image, so the politicians had a pretty free hand in dealing with us. Not only were we lousy administrators, we were also seen as the cosseted inhabitants of ivory towers, immune to the realities of the real world, diddling away at research on obscure topics without any contemporary relevance and publishing books and articles every so often that were of interest only to other academics. We, as well as the universities that employed us, had to be "modernized".

Jameson took a final sip of coffee and sat back in his chair. 'I teach a course on "managing change in the workplace" and it soon occurred to me that a pretty classic case study was occurring before my eyes. Not all in one fell swoop, of course. That would have violated all the precepts of change management. No, it started gradually, almost sympathetically, with a few questionnaires from our central administration about workloads, work-related stress and the like. The administration seemed to be on our side then, as buffeted and bewildered by new government initiatives as most of us academics were. That was stage 1. Then what's known as the "unsettling" phase began, as our administrators realized that there was an important funding game to be played and they had no choice but to play it. First, some attempts at mission statements at the university and faculty level, just to familiarize us with the new vocabulary of corporate "audit" culture. Next a series of highly critical internal reports, most of them picked up by the media, about the "inefficiencies" of tutorial teaching, "insufficiently rigorous" training of graduate students, and "resistance to new approaches to knowledge transmission" in some university departments. These were intended to stir up debate and dissension, and that they did. To achieve change in any organization, it is essential not only to discredit the status quo, but also to de-stabilize the work force, to make it clear that there will be losers as well as winners, and to provide those who would be winners with a road map to the future. Every few years there was a research assessment exercise and teaching assessment exercise at the faculty level, and faculties themselves were reviewed in turn. Much of this was mandated by the state, but more and more of it was internally generated by our new management tier. After all, these people had been employed to maximize Exton's state funding, and they had to earn their keep. We were inundated with questionnaires then about how many students we taught, how many "contact hours" we had with them, how much of our time we spent on research and administration. Stage 2 was in full swing.

'It was at that point, a little over two years ago, that HEFCE announced it was going to take a new approach to allocating research funding in future, a Research Excellence Framework that would also reward universities for the broader "impacts" of the research their academic staff carried out. This ushered in stage 3 in change management here at Exton and elsewhere. Previously, it had been only the *quality* of research that counted, as determined by panels of academic experts in the disciplines concerned, and the higher the assessed quality of a university's constituent parts, the larger the state grant it received. Now there would also be significant financial rewards for those universities who could prove that their research was benefitting the UK economy and "national well-being". Since every university already had a management tier in place and the managers within that tier had a personal as well as professional stake in getting their institutions to perform as well as possible in the funding frenzies that took place at regular intervals, HEFCE could simply establish some very general guidelines and leave it to them to nurture the "units of assessment" that would count in future. The appraisal scheme is a key part of Exton's response to that challenge.'

'I guess I can see how economic impact might be measured,' Akiko said. 'Some finding that leads to a new technology, resulting in new business and job opportunities.

We hear a lot about that sort of thing in Japan. But what about national well-being?'

'Another good question,' Sir Christopher replied. 'That's going to be a particularly tricky area, especially when it comes to impacts on "culture and the quality of life" within that sphere. The impacts have to be "demonstrable", according to HEFCE, but how does one demonstrate, say, the impact of a study of George Eliot or, to cite an example closer to your home and mine, of the study of poverty in contemporary Japan that a TH fellow has just completed? Even in the more easily quantifiable economic sphere, how does one prove that a single science or engineering cluster within a given university was solely responsible for the beneficial outcome subsequently observed? Litigation over the ownership of that outcome is highly likely, given that there are substantial sums of funding in the balance. I suspect, too, that academics in all disciplines are going to have to pay much greater attention to externally defined research agendas in future, issues that others beyond academe have defined as worthy of investigation, rather than to their own knowledge-driven curiosity, and they're going to have to keep all sorts of new records to help in quantifying the impact their research has. No doubt our managers will be keeping close tabs on those agendas and encouraging our research clusters to do the same. And they'll get a push in that direction from the "experts" and the research "users" who are going to evaluate submissions. There's no mention of "peer review" in HEFCE's new plan. It's "expert review" now, and that means people who not only know the disciplines concerned but also the supposed wider uses and benefits of it. They're going to be supplemented by research users, a rather vaguely defined category but one that is certain to include people from commerce and industry.'

'You're right about that, Chris,' said Jameson. 'And you're also right that impacts are hard to assess. I gather that some time lag will be permitted – say, ten years or so between the time the research was undertaken and its impact clear enough to measure. But in the meantime this university is using all sorts of proxy indicators to build its case for the future: external research funding received, publication of research findings in leading journals, the number of references to those findings made by other researchers, highly visible media coverage of diverse sorts. Giving a 90-second interview on some radio or TV programme now counts for more than a good review in an academic journal. We have mid-level managers who will help in arranging that. They're doing PR, but like the rest of us they're responsible to the accountants at higher levels. The accountants have taken over Exton. I expect it is pretty much the same elsewhere.'

'So you share the Warden's misgivings about the new appraisal scheme?' Akiko asked.

'Oh yes,' replied Jameson. 'It reminds me of some of the Taylorist scientific management efforts to boost the productivity of shop-floor labour that I read about back in my student days. Of course, I've been convinced for years that our universities, this one in particular, need a better way of rewarding merit. Note that I said "merit", not "productivity". Universities aren't factories, at least not yet.'

'Dr Chang seemed upset about definitions of productivity,' Akiko observed. 'He said that nothing he had published recently counted as research.'

Jameson sighed. 'I don't recall that we practitioners were

ever asked for our definitions of research,' he said. 'A pretty simplistic science-based model – conduct a controlled experiment about some new or poorly understood phenomenon and write up the results – was ordained from on high. "Evidence-based research" suddenly became the order of the day, our new mantra. Speculation was out, as were reflection, interpretation and synthesis, even though some of the most innovative and transformative ideas have come from scholarly works of those sorts in the past. And translations of works from other languages were also out. Even if they open up new worlds of experience to us, the original texts are by definition "old", there for the taking, as it were. Nothing credibly innovative about doing that. Amanda, my wife, now dashes off one or two "evidence-based" articles about the careers of little-known composers every summer, just so she can continue organizing workshops on vocal and instrumental polyphony in term time. She's made some intriguing findings, but not at the rate or of the sort that will raise her score under the proposed new regime.'

'And Professor Bates?' asked Akiko. 'Am I right that he was opposed to the proposed new regime?'

'You can be sure of that,' Jameson replied. 'I just hope that all the effort Theo put into opposing it didn't contribute to his untimely death.'

* * *

In a pub not far from TH that same lunchtime, Tom and Sanderson sat at a corner table with three of the students Tom had spoken with the night before.

'So you two go way back, then,' said Michelle Barton, a

PhD student in Anthropology, after Tom had introduced Sanderson. 'That's good. I've sort of lost touch with everyone I went to school with.'

'I hope it doesn't take a murder to get me back in touch with my high school pals,' said Bill Jenkins, an American from Virginia who was midway through a two-year Master's course in Russian Studies.

'What makes you think we're dealing with a homicide?' Sanderson asked.

'Well, to start off with,' Jenkins replied, 'I'm sitting here with you, and you are a policeman. Why else would you want to see us?'

'It's just routine, whenever there's an unexplained death,' Sanderson said, trying to look reassuring. 'I just need some background on Professor Bates. What sort of a person he was, his place in the college, things like that.'

'He was a great guy,' said Adam Brown, who was close to completing his doctoral thesis in modern Balkan history, and the others nodded in assent. 'He always had time to talk with students, even those in fields other than history. We felt he was, well, on our side in all the debate about reform that has been raging recently.'

'Like changing the requirements for the doctorate,' Barton said with considerable vigour. 'Some of the dons here have been talking about doing away with the PhD thesis. "Why train students to complete a book-length study," they say, "when the book is finished. Better to train them how to write articles." There's already a degree programme in one of the faculties here that specifies three articles accepted for publication in peer-reviewed journals as an alternative to a 100,000-word thesis. That, they say, would bring us into line with the scientists, who have been writing 30 to 40,000-word doctoral theses for donkeys-years. And there's even been talk about cutting down the time that can be funded for research or fieldwork abroad from a year to no more than six months. Okay, we anthropologists probably don't need a whole calendar year in the field anymore, now that we've practically run out of "previously unknown" tribal cultures to study, whose behaviour during, say, the rising moon of the 12th month just might provide the key to their entire social system. But I certainly need more than six months in Bangalore to carry out the call-centre ethnography I'm planning for my thesis. It will take at least two months just to make contact and establish rapport with useful informants. Bates understood that, and he encouraged me to apply for the fieldwork funding I need while I still have a chance of getting it. My supervisor says she's on my side, too, but she has so many students to look after she really doesn't have time to run through the funding options with me, much less to critique my draft applications.'

'Same with my supervisor,' said Jenkins. 'He had ten students to look after last year; this year he has twenty. And I have to make an appointment at least two weeks in advance whenever I want to see him. I'm doing my master's thesis on commemoration of the Gulag in post-Soviet Russia, and it's slowing me down to have to wait so long for advice. I had been thinking about doing a PhD and pursuing an academic career, but now I just want to get out of here with a decent degree in a year's time and maybe get a job in journalism or even diplomacy. That way I might be able to spend more time in Russia than I would as an academic.'

Brown listened to Jenkins with a wry smile and said, 'I'm

too far gone now to take Bill's route. I'm submitting my thesis next month, and I've already got an academic job lined up for September. Not here, though. In the States. I talked it over with Bates when I was deciding between the two offers I had, one here and one there. I think he was disappointed that I opted for leaving the UK, but he did say that at least I'd have to publish another book over there, if I wanted to get tenure. He urged me to keep in touch, and now, now he's gone.'

'To Professor Bates,' said Barton, lifting her near-empty glass of beer. 'He is going to be sorely missed.'

All the others raised their glasses. Then Tom thanked them for coming, and they went their separate ways.

CHAPTER 5

It was 2.35. Baxter was about to send Sanderson out in search of his last interviewee of the day when there was a loud knock on the door and a tall, thin man in a well-tailored beige linen suit entered the room. His wavy silvery-white hair was neatly brushed back, his thick white eyebrows elegantly combed, his face deeply lined but tanned.

'My apologies for keeping you waiting,' he said, 'but I had to see the Domestic Bursar about Bates's room.' He eased himself into the chair opposite Baxter, carefully leaning his cane against his right knee. 'I'm Winston Avery-Hill, and you must be DCI Baxter. I'm a bit pressed for time, but I'll answer any questions you care to ask.'

'Thank you, Professor,' Baxter responded coolly. 'DC Sanderson here will take notes,' he added, gesturing toward his younger colleague whom Avery-Hill had so far ignored. 'I do have several questions, but let's start with your visit just now to the Domestic Bursar. What is it about Bates's room you needed to discuss?'

Avery-Hill looked surprised. 'Whether it could be redecorated before I go off on holiday in late August,' he answered. 'It's too good a room to be given to just anybody, so I've laid claim to it. Too bad about Bates, of course, but I'm the Senior Fellow now.'

Baxter glanced at one of the papers on the table in front of him. 'Am I right that your current room is directly above Bates's room?' he asked.

'That's right,' said Avery-Hill. 'But it doesn't get any shade from that puny cherry tree in the garden below, and so it gets pretty hot up there in summer. Not that the heat has slowed me down – I've topped the output list in my department for years, not to mention the Google league table within TH. But Bates's room is cooler, and that should boost my productivity even further.' He tapped his right knee. 'Good for this old fellow, too. Still fine for walking and pacing, but neither of us likes stairs.'

'Ah yes, the pacing,' said Baxter. 'I gather that was a source of friction between you and Bates.'

Avery-Hill stiffened. 'There were many sources of friction between us, but that was the least of them. Bates was against change in academe. I am its champion. Everyone in Exton knows that. But I fail to see how any of this relates to your enquiry. Surely you are not suggesting that I something to do with his death?'

'I am not suggesting anything,' Baxter responded. 'Just getting the background information we need on Bates's movements during the past few days, his state of mind, things like that. You may have heard that he left a note on his desk?' Avery-Hill nodded. 'So what do you make of it?' Baxter asked. 'What was so "terribly wrong", what was "the answer"?'

'It's all a complete mystery to me,' said Avery-Hill sharply. 'Nothing to do with my pacing, I can assure you. That's how I compose, on my feet and onto tape. It makes for punchier, more memorable prose. If the occasional creaking floorboard above his head bothered him so much, he should have switched rooms with me, as I suggested long ago. And just how, may I ask, did this trivial matter come to your attention?'

Baxter felt pleased with the tension he had generated in the interview thus far, but merely smiled blandly. 'From the emails between Bates and you,' he answered, reaching for the stack of print-outs to his left. 'Let's see, yes, here's the first one I wanted to ask you about. On November 18th Bates emailed you that he had "found yet another of your new graduate students collapsed in tears at the foot of the stairs". What's that all about?'

Avery-Hill raised one of his luxuriant eyebrows and leaned forward intently. 'I'll tell you what it's about! It's about the only sensible approach to graduate training,' he replied, looking straight at Baxter. 'Undergraduates are like sponges, you know. They absorb what their teachers tell them. Then some of them get admitted to graduate school, and they think they already know their subject. Well, they don't. Plenty of students apply to study with me – I have fifteen doctoral students at present, compared to Bates's measly five, you know – and they're pretty full of themselves at the outset, having been accepted here despite the competition for places and then getting me as their supervisor. Well, the first thing I do is to squeeze their sponges dry. I take each one of them through the sample papers and the research proposal they submitted with their application, and I point out all their errors in conceptualization and argument. Then I assign them a topic to write on for our next meeting, and I tear that to shreds, too. Some resist longer than others, but eventually they all crack. It might take two, or even three, essays in some cases, but I'm not "Winston the Ripper" for nothing. I make them all crack. The tears that so upset Bates are a sign that they are finally ready to do proper graduate work under my direction.'

'So why was Bates upset?' asked Baxter.

'Bates was old-fashioned in the extreme,' Avery-Hill replied with more than a hint of a sneer in his voice. 'He coddled his graduate students. Why, if he felt he didn't know enough about the research a new student proposed to carry out, he'd spend hours reading up on the topic, and then even more time in helping the student to refine the project. That's no way to advance knowledge! Maybe it doesn't matter in a useless field like medieval history, but it certainly matters in mine. We do cutting-edge research, after all. We deal with issues that affect the future of the entire world. I've been to three UN conferences and four EU conferences on international conflict resolution in the past year alone! I've been on "Newsnight" twice since Easter! We can't afford to let egotistical young graduate students do whatever research they want. They may be bright, but they have to be stripped of all their preconceived ideas before they're ready to make significant contributions to the field.'

Baxter resisted the urge to ask when international conflict might be expected to come to an end. 'Right,' he said calmly. 'Thanks for that explanation. Let's turn now to selection of the next Arkwright Post-doctoral Fellow. Bates emailed you on February 17th to report that that he had just received a copy of the original reference submitted by Professor Atkinson for Dr Anna Ponti and it differed in one key respect from the reference circulated earlier to the selection committee. Atkinson's original reference, according to Bates, stated that her proposed research project "was particularly innovative, and when completed it is likely to have a major impact on the field". The letter sent to the committee stated that her project "was not particularly innovative, but if completed successfully it would certainly advance knowledge in the field". You chaired that committee, and all the references were sent to you as email attachments in the first instance. Bates asked you for clarification, but you don't appear to have replied.'

Avery-Hill was now sitting bolt upright, his face slightly flushed. 'I was not about to dignify his thinly veiled assault on my integrity with a reply, that's why you didn't find one!' he snapped. 'Atkinson is a medievalist like Bates, you know. No doubt both of them were upset their candidate didn't get invited to interview, but the truth is there were plenty of better qualified applicants. There was even one in archaeology, as I recall. It's not my problem if some scholars don't know how to write appropriate references.'

'But it was one of your former doctoral students who got the post-doc, was it not?' asked Baxter.

'Yes, it was,' replied Avery-Hill, staring coldly at Baxter. 'By a majority of those on the selection committee, I might add. Only Bates and one other TH fellow voted against.' He reached for his cane. 'I'm afraid I have nothing more to contribute here…'

'Just a couple more questions, Professor,' Baxter said. 'Do please remain seated and tell me when you last saw Bates.'

Avery-Hill frowned but slowly placed his cane back against his knee. 'It must have been last Saturday. Yes, I'm sure of that,' he said. 'I came in mid-morning to collect some off-prints of my latest article so I could distribute them at a conference I was attending. They weren't on my desk, so I headed off to the Porters' Lodge to see if my secretary had left them in my pigeonhole instead. Bates was coming up the path just as I went out the door. I expect we exchanged greetings, can't say I remember exactly, but we certainly didn't have a conversation. I collected my off-prints, went back to my room for my briefcase and headed home. I left for the conference in Brussels on Sunday afternoon, and I didn't get back to Exton until about midnight on Tuesday. The next thing I heard about Bates was the telephone call I received from the Bursar last night, summoning me to an interview with you today.'

'That's very helpful,' Baxter said. 'Just one or two final questions. You mentioned the Google league table a while back. Am I right that you and Bates had some disagreements about that, too?'

A guarded look came over Avery-Hill's face. 'It's just a little game I play. I google all the TH fellows on May Day every year and then rank them by the number of their entries. It sort of gets the competitive juices flowing, you know, and it might even get some of the less productive fellows into shape for the new appraisal drill. I make it a point to inform everyone of his or her score. You could say I'm doing them a favour.'

'And you've always topped the rankings?'

'That's correct. I suspect Bates was jealous of that.' Avery-Hill shifted his weight in the chair.

Baxter turned to the final marked page in the off-prints in front of him. 'So you think it was jealousy that led him to include some of your articles in his testing of the new CrossCheck software for the journal he edited?' he asked. 'Apparently your "originality" scores were quite low, with an average of 38 per cent of the text in each article replicated without citation from one or more of your previous publications. I gather that's called "self-plagiarism", and it's of growing concern within academic circles these days.'

'Utter nonsense!' Avery-Hill retorted. 'So there's a bit of overlap between what I wrote a few years ago and some of my most recent publications. In the social sciences we often use the same data over and over again. The interpretations change, but there's bound to be some replication of the core material. When it comes to interpretations I can assure you that I am very original indeed, and the leading journals in my field are always delighted to publish my work.'

'And what about plagiarism of the more traditional sort?' Baxter now asked. 'In an email on June 1st Bates informs you that some 25 per cent of the text in one of your recent articles duplicates the text in an online working paper by one of your graduate students back in 2002. Unfortunately the student died in a road accident before he finished his thesis, which by all reports was going to be quite brilliant. Bates wonders if you plan to use more of his work in advancing your own career. What do you say to that?'

Avery-Hill thrust himself to his feet, turned toward the door and immediately toppled over.

Sanderson phoned 999 for an ambulance while Baxter bent over Avery-Hill's crumpled body and began the standard resuscitation drill.

CHAPTER 6

Akiko, Sir Christopher and the Bursar, David Stitch, had been having tea in the Warden's Garden when Baxter arrived a little after 4.15 pm. Akiko had offered to leave, but Sir Christopher insisted she stay. 'You may as well hear the latest in this sorry tale,' he said with a wan smile. 'Do sit down, Inspector,' he continued. 'What news of Winston?'

'The paramedics say he hyperventilated,' Baxter replied, accepting a cup of tea from Akiko. 'That's "fainted" to us ordinary folk. Because of his recent heart trouble, they've taken him up to the hospital for some more tests, but they're pretty sure he can go home tonight. They said he should be fine after a few days' rest.'

'My secretary phoned Daphne as soon as we learned what had happened,' the Bursar said. 'That's Mrs Avery-Hill,' he added, looking first at Akiko and then at Baxter. 'I'm afraid she had some harsh words to say about "police bullying tactics", but she'll get over it soon, I'm sure. She should be up at the hospital now.'

Sir Christopher sighed. 'I'll telephone her this evening. Maybe I can calm her down a bit.'

'Heart trouble seems to have been the only thing those two professors had in common,' Baxter observed. 'And each of them had one of those new INR devices to help him monitor his medications. We've just discovered that those devices had been exchanged. Bates had Avery-Hill's, and vice versa. We don't yet know exactly when that happened, but we're checking out a lead.'

There was a stunned silence, as Baxter had anticipated. 'Perhaps you'd like to hear what else we've learned to date?' he asked. 'By means of normal procedures, of course,' he added. 'We don't "do bullying".'

Sir Christopher slowly put down his tea cup and leaned back in his chair. His face was ashen, but his voice was firm when he spoke. 'Mrs Avery-Hill tends to over-react at the best of times,' he said. 'We certainly do not share her views, and we'd appreciate hearing your findings. Everyone at TH wants this matter resolved as quickly as possible.'

Baxter nodded and launched into an account of the investigation so far, starting with the reports of the IT technician and the Chief Pathologist and ending with his questioning of Avery-Hill.

Akiko was the first to speak after he had finished. 'Professor Bates seems to have gone to great lengths to die at his desk in College.'

'Quite right, Ms Sugiyama,' said Baxter, casting an appreciative glance in her direction. 'Frankly, I'm surprised he risked the trip to York. He'd been without warfarin for at least a month – our constable found close to fifty tablets stuffed into one of the desk drawers at his house – and he must have known that his chances of a fatal heart attack were increasing with every passing day. We've checked with the local taxi firms. One of them picked up an elderly male passenger at the station at 8.30 on Tuesday night and let him off at the top of School Lane a few minutes later. We assume that the passenger was Bates and that he went directly to his room and remained there overnight. His suitcase was still there when he was found yesterday afternoon, and there's no sign that he'd been at his house since Monday morning. The scout who cleans that wing of the Fellows' Building says that they only empty the waste bins in work rooms on Tuesdays, Wednesdays and Fridays. She wasn't surprised to find Bates's door unlocked – apparently that happened fairly often. She could see from the doorway that the bin was empty and left, locking the door behind her with her pass key. Bates could well have been sitting in the easy chair behind the door, and she wouldn't have seen him.'

'But why would Bates come back to College?' the Bursar asked. 'Surely he should have gone straight to A&E if he was feeling unwell.'

Sir Christopher sighed. 'As Akiko says, he wanted to die at his desk. Leaving a cryptic note, so that the police would get involved. That was the only way to make sure you examined his computer, wasn't it?' he asked, looking at Baxter.

Baxter hesitated only slightly. 'Well, if he'd died elsewhere and the note had come to our attention later, we might have become interested,' he replied. 'Bates probably left the note on his desk before he headed for York. Maybe he had left it there for a week or more. But there's no doubt that the combination of his corpse and the note right there on the desk in front of it had greater impact. It was pretty good staging, and it worked. By the way, I'm pretty sure it was Bates who exchanged the INR devices. At any rate, he had an opportunity to do so on Saturday, when he encountered Avery-Hill dashing to the Lodge. As I see it, Bates figured Avery-Hill might have left the door to his room open, and when he found that to be the case he took advantage of it. It was an added flourish he couldn't resist.'

'An added flourish.' Sir Christopher repeated the phrase in a solemn tone. 'Bates could have come to me with his suspicions, you know. He could have shown me his email records. We do have a disciplinary procedure in this college, after all. I'm not sure what we could have done about Winston's treatment of his students without a complaint from at least one of them, but I certainly would have wanted to investigate the allegations about plagiarism and tampering with references further. Why didn't Bates see that? Why this theatrical staging of his demise? I can only think of it as a gesture of no confidence, in me primarily, and then in the fellowship.'

'There is the Google league table issue,' the Bursar said quietly. 'Governing Body decided two years ago that it was an anti-collegial practice, especially as Winston was prone to chide those with low scores both privately and in public, and he was asked to give it up, or at least to keep his tallies to himself in future. It would appear from what DCI Baxter has told us, however, that he failed to abide by this request. No one complained to you, so you didn't know. Our procedures assume compliance with the general will. I suppose one could say they are flawed in that respect. Maybe Bates realized that only a dramatic gesture would get our attention to the issues as he saw them.'

'He was very ill,' Baxter added. 'His consultant was unaware that he'd stopped taking the warfarin, of course, but still he was not surprised by the news that Bates had died. He says he had told Bates only last May that his prognosis was not at all positive. Bates had just shrugged and said it was a good thing he was working on the conclusion to his book. "Still time to get my affairs in order," he'd said, and that was the last conversation they had.'

'Does it make any difference that the police now know about the issues that concerned Professor Bates?' asked Akiko.

To the relief of both the Warden and Bursar, Baxter shook his head. 'This is no longer a matter of concern to the police,' he said. 'We did what was necessary at the outset, when confronted with a suspicious death, but I'm sure the Coroner will now sign a death certificate on the basis of the Chief Pathologist's report and my report: Professor Bates died from a massive heart attack, likely to have happened at any time but almost certainly hastened by his failure to take his prescribed medication. Whatever further steps are taken in connection with the issues he raised are entirely up to the College.'

'I will be having a conversation with Winston as soon as he's able,' said Sir Christopher, rising to his feet. 'It's obvious we have a few matters to clear up, and they will be cleared up, I assure you. But now I'd like to thank you for your prompt, and I would add, very sensible, resolution of this tragic affair.'

The Bursar and Akiko, too, stood up, and there were handshakes all around. Baxter took his leave. Akiko collected the tea things on a tray and headed across the lawn toward the Lodgings. Sir Christopher and the Bursar exchanged a few words about arrangements for TKA4's visit and agreed that a memorial service for Bates should be scheduled for mid-October, soon after the start of the new academic year.

Just four days later these same people would again be having tea in this very same garden and discussing a further, and definitely more suspicious, death.

CHAPTER 7

After putting the tea cups into the dishwasher, Akiko went back to the library and resumed the restoration work she had begun that morning. She had just applied a thin layer of epoxy to the edges of the final, tiny fragment when Tom came in about 6.30.

'Hey, it's a vase again!' he exclaimed.

Akiko pressed the fragment into place, held it for a moment and then sat back. She removed her face mask and smiled. 'Not quite yet,' she said. 'The glue has to dry for at least four days. Seven would be better, but we don't have that long. Then there's a lot of polishing to be done to get rid of all traces of the glue, and finally some painting. See here, in the centre? I'll have to touch up these petals on the peony motif. And up here, too, on this butterfly. Hmm, there's a flaw in this leaf, too. And here. The more one looks, the more one finds! If I do the polishing Monday night and the painting first thing Tuesday morning, we should be all right. When does the display case arrive? What time does TKA4 arrive on Wednesday?' She poured a thick layer of horticultural sand into a plastic washing-up bowl as she spoke and delicately settled the reconstructed vase onto the sand. Then she tore off two long strips of micropore tape and laid each one over the top of the vase, securing the ends tightly to the sides of the bowl.

'I'm picking up the display case on Monday,' Tom replied, 'so there's no worry on that score. With TKA4, it's always hard to tell. We expected him late afternoon last year, but he arrived just before lunch. He said he'd finished up all his business in London at a breakfast meeting and "had nothing better to do but head straight for his favourite Exton college". Fortunately, Dad was in his office, and I expect he'll be there all morning this year. The Chef is likely to have a nice lunch at the ready, too.'

'Right,' said Akiko, removing her gloves. 'We'll be ready for him, whenever he comes. But you must take the vase out of the display case right after he leaves and let it sit in a cool, dimly lit room for a week so the enamel will harden properly.' She stood up and stretched. 'Is now a good time to visit your studio?' she asked.

Tom laughed nervously. 'It's hardly a studio,' he said, 'just part of the basement here. There are two window wells, so the light's not bad, especially not at this time of year. But if you're too tired...'

'I am not tired at all,' she replied cheerily, 'and both of us need to get out of this room as soon as possible, before the glue gets to us. It's the perfect time, really.'

Tom led the way down the narrow stairs off the kitchen and opened the basement door. The lingering sunset of an English summer's day was already well underway, and a pale golden glow infused the room. Akiko looked around, noting that an old leather armchair was placed just to the right of the window well directly ahead of her, with a plump cushion nestled invitingly at its back. There was a jam jar containing a few pink roses on the rickety table next to the chair and other signs of recent efforts at making the space presentable: an overflowing waste bin by the door, an array of watercolours on the work table in the darker interior of the room, numerous canvases lined up rather too neatly against the wall beyond the work table. On an easel just a few feet from the basement door was a large sketch pad, its open page facing toward the leather chair.

'This looks like a very proper garret to me,' Akiko said from the doorway, 'even if it is mostly underground! Is that some work in progress on the easel?'

'Go have a look,' Tom replied.

Akiko took a few steps forward, peered at the sketch pad and giggled. 'It's a good likeness, I have to admit,' she said, once she'd regained her composure. 'Everyone says I frown like that when I'm concentrating. And I wasn't even aware you were sketching me. I'd say it was just after lunch yesterday, to judge from the state of the fragments. You know, the hands are very good. Somehow I thought you specialized in landscapes, but obviously you've done a lot of life studies, too. Have you taken classes?'

'I did take a class in London last summer,' said Tom, 'but mostly I work on people closer to home.' He turned back a few pages in the sketch pad. 'Here's Dad reading the paper earlier this week.'

'Not a good news day, was it?' Akiko observed. 'Or do you specialize in frowns? You have certainly captured his mildly exasperated look.'

'Do take a seat,' Tom replied. 'Over there in the only decent chair down here, and I'll show you something a bit different.' He opened another sketch pad and placed it on the easel. 'Here's Lucy,' he said quietly. 'She is smiling, as usual.'

Akiko felt a twinge of regret that she had sat down as

directed. Had she remained standing by the easel, she could have reached out and touched Tom. Now there was a space between them, a buffer that required words not gestures. On the easel was a sketch of his twelve-year-old sister, eyes sparkling, laughing – and dead from meningitis these past three years.

'Oh, Tom,' she said after a moment. 'It's a lovely sketch. You must miss her very much.'

Now it was Tom's turn to frown, ever so slightly. 'I've been thinking about yesterday morning, when we were out on the river bank. Why haven't I got over it by now?' He retrieved a small painting from the work table and placed it on the easel. 'Here she is in watercolours. This is my favourite, but done from memory like all the rest of my attempts. It never occurred to me to paint her while she was alive.'

Akiko sighed. 'It never occurred to me to tell my husband I loved him on the morning he set off on his last ever motorcycle trip,' she said. 'He was just going into town to pick up some supplies. I punished myself for my failure for months. But finally I realized that no one can be blamed for being unable to predict the future. You can't be blamed, mustn't blame yourself, either. And just look again at the subtle colours you've used in that portrait, not only for her hair and complexion, but for the background, too. She is surrounded by dawn, isn't she? Maybe remembering her, trying to recapture her on paper, has something to do with your fascination with light.'

Tom placed another, larger painting on the easel. 'I've been working on sunsets recently,' he said. 'Maybe it's a healthy sign?'

'That's very dramatic,' Akiko replied. 'Almost unsettling.

Will the sequel be a thunderstorm?'

Tom reached for the swivel chair at the work table, turned it toward Akiko and sat down. 'Actually, I had been thinking of a thunderstorm, but the truth is I haven't been able to get started on it. Except for a few sketches – you, Dad, the scout who comes in to clean every morning – I haven't done any work in over a week. I'm feeling drained.'

Akiko nodded. 'Will you tell me why you blame your mother for Lucy's death?' she asked. She was relieved to see that Tom relaxed back into his chair.

'I was in Cambridge, just about to finish my second year,' he began, 'and Dad was at an alumni do in New York. Lucy came down with a fever on the Friday night, so my mother put her to bed. The fever was a bit higher on Saturday morning, but my mother and one of her London friends had tickets for a special viewing of the new exhibit at the Royal Gallery and off she went. She told Eric, the student she'd hired to look after Lucy that day, to telephone her if there were any problems, but then she forgot to turn her mobile on. And after the exhibit she and her friend went shopping and then to dinner at some posh restaurant. Eric tried to phone her several times. He had become increasingly concerned about Lucy – her fever stayed high, and she just lay in her bed all limp and dazed – so finally he phoned NHS Direct, and after they heard about her symptoms they told him to call an ambulance straight away. That was early afternoon. Lucy went into a coma on the way to hospital and died early the next morning. The doctor said he might have been able to save her if she'd been brought in just a few hours earlier. My mother blamed Eric at first, and then the doctor. She got more and more hysterical, and a few days later she

59

went to pieces. As well she might have. It was her fault for not being there. For not even checking to make sure her damned phone was switched on.'

'And you?' Akiko asked. 'How did you hear about Lucy?'

'I got a call from the Bursar a little after 4.00 on Saturday,' Tom replied. 'Eric had phoned the Lodge right after he'd phoned for an ambulance, and the porter on duty immediately rang David at home. He contacted my father first, I guess. I borrowed a friend's car and got to the hospital just before 8.00. My mother didn't get there until about midnight. Dad got on the earliest flight he could and David met him at Heathrow first thing the next morning, but they were about half an hour too late.' Tom had wiped away a tear with the back of his hand earlier on, but now tears were streaming down his cheeks.

'You must have felt so helpless,' Akiko said softly.

'They wouldn't let me into Lucy's room,' Tom sobbed. 'I just stood at the window for hours looking in at her, lying there motionless. They tried to keep my mother out, too, when she finally arrived, but she just swept past them, wailing "What have they done to my darling little girl?" She didn't even notice me.'

'Oh Tom,' Akiko murmured, reaching out toward him. He thrust himself out of his chair and buried his face in her lap. She stroked his head and his shoulders until he stopped crying.

'I don't expect your father paid much attention to you either,' she said eventually.

Tom now sat cross-legged on the floor at her feet, his face resting against her knees. 'No,' he said sadly. 'He had his hands full dealing with my mother. I went back to Cambridge right after the funeral for exams, and then I spent the summer wandering around Italy with a couple of my friends. By the time I got home in late September my parents had already split up. She's back in France somewhere, I think. She hasn't been in touch with me.'

'And has your father seen your portrait of Lucy?' Akiko asked.

Tom sat up. 'It would just bring all the pain back, wouldn't it?' he asked. 'His as well as mine.'

'Sometimes that's the best thing,' Akiko replied, 'especially when the pain has been buried in the first place. But it's up to you. Think about it. Okay?'

Tom got to his feet slowly and wiped his face with a paint-stained cloth from the nearby work table. 'Okay,' he said. 'Sorry about all that.'

'Now you're going British on me again!' Akiko chided him. 'Stop apologizing and either show me some more of your paintings or take me out to supper.'

Tom smiled his engaging smile, showed her lots more of his paintings and then bought her a good dinner at a Chinese restaurant in the city centre. Sir Christopher was reading at the kitchen table when they finally arrived back at the Lodgings. 'Hello there, you two,' he boomed. 'I took a peek into the library when I finally made it home an hour ago, and I figured you had cause to head off and celebrate. It's a vase again! I commend you. We'll be ready for TKA4, no matter when he arrives on Wednesday!'

Tom and Akiko burst out laughing at almost precisely the same moment and happily agreed to join the Warden in his special summer nightcap.

'So what's next?' Sir Christopher asked as he spooned

crushed ice into three tall glasses and poured his secret concoction of liqueurs and fruit juices on top, finishing off each glass with a sprig of mint from the plant on the kitchen windowsill. College rumour had it that several North Exton ladies of a certain age competed with one another to keep him supplied with the home-made apple cider that was a key ingredient.

Akiko explained the remaining restoration drill and said, 'So I'll head off to Paris tomorrow to meet with some of my colleagues there. I'm booked on the Eurostar at noon, and then I head back to London a little after noon on Monday. I should be back in Exton by teatime at the latest.'

'We can take the 9.35 train to London together,' Sir Christopher said, beaming. 'I'm going to an afternoon seminar at Chatham House, and I have a few errands to run beforehand. Tom can drive us to the station a little after 9.00.'

Akiko made a mental note to point out to him that he was treating his son like a servant, but for the moment she just smiled and said, 'Tom may have other plans for the morning, so perhaps we should book a taxi?'

'No plans,' Tom said quickly. 'I'll have the car at the door at 9.05, and I'll loan Akiko my Oyster card so she doesn't have to queue for a tube ticket at Paddington.'

'Fine!' Sir Christopher answered, refilling their glasses with the remainder of his concoction. 'Now drink up, both of you, and then we should all be off to bed. It's way past 11.00. I will provide us all with coffee and toast at 8.15 sharp tomorrow morning.'

CHAPTER 8

'We're in luck!' exclaimed Sir Christopher as the train to London pulled into Exton Station right on time the next morning and came slowly to a halt. 'There's an older carriage just up there, with private compartments. So much more civilized than the newer carriages, don't you think?' He steered Akiko up the platform some forty feet and helped her on board. 'Ah yes,' he said as they made their way along the narrow corridor. 'Why sit in serried rows within earshot of everyone else's conversation and the swishing bass notes of their music when you can enjoy a bit of sanctuary? And all at the second-class fare that the Bursar allows me to claim on my expenses.' He soon spied an empty compartment and ushered Akiko inside. 'Do you wish a forward- or a backward-facing seat, my dear?' he asked.

Akiko chose backward-facing and smiled as the Warden sat down opposite her, a foot or so from the window, and carefully placed his briefcase and newspaper in the space remaining to his left. 'I can see you are an expert at occupying these compartments to the full,' she said, stroking the worn velvet upholstery on the space next to her. 'Very nostalgic. I'm afraid we've only had serried rows in Japanese trains for decades now. Safer for lone travellers, especially women, we're told, but probably more profitable for the operators as they can fit more seats into every carriage. The usual mix of motives, I suppose.'

'The same thing is happening here, for the same reasons,' Sir Christopher said, 'but at our usual slower pace. Old codgers like me should be all right for another few years, and by the time the rolling stock on this line has been completely replaced I expect I will have stepped down from the wardenship and escaped to my rural retreat to enjoy the simple life for a change.'

'Where is your rural retreat?' Akiko asked, finding it rather difficult to imagine Sir Christopher in anything but an urban setting.

'In my imagination, alas,' Sir Christopher replied. 'I'm not even sure which country it's in, but I have a small house in Notting Hill that I've owned since the early 1970s which I'm hoping to sell for a vast sum, and then I'll go off in search of it. I'll set aside a bit of the profit for Tom, of course, but he can't expect me to support him forever.'

Akiko decided that it would be wiser to start talking about the Warden's quest for a simple life and then to move on to the subject of Tom. 'So you've been finding things difficult at TH even before the recent tragic event?' she asked.

'The first three years or so were wonderful,' Sir Christopher said. 'The College Governing Body listened avidly to my every word and instantly agreed to almost all of my suggestions. What a pleasant change from the Foreign Office! But then these reform initiatives began to bite – the "unsettling phase" that Jameson mentioned yesterday – and tensions within the fellowship started mounting. I began getting turgid memos of complaint and late-night phone calls from some of the fellows, and even the simplest proposal for, say, replacing a tree in the main quad, led to controversy. Get a bunch of academics together, and it's quite amazing what hitherto unexamined aspects of arboriculture are likely to surface. I began to feel more like a referee than a head of house, but that said, some of my fellow heads of house have told me it's par for the course these days. Deference of the old sort for a few years, then the grumbling starts, and the next kind words one hears are at one's retirement dinner. I signed on for ten years, so with only a little over two years to go I'm already virtually a lame duck. A committee to find my successor will be formed early next year. Bates would have chaired it, as the Senior Fellow. Good God, it's going to be Avery-Hill now!' Sir Christopher stiffened as this realization sank in. 'That man is a menace to collegiality,' he said after a brief pause, 'and the less he has to do with the future of TH, the better. I think I'll have to be a bit firmer with him about his misdeeds than I might have been otherwise and a bit careless in keeping our conversation confidential. Fortunately, it is next to impossible to keep anything secret within an Exton college.'

'What exactly do you mean by collegiality?' Akiko asked.

Sir Christopher relaxed back into his seat. 'You've heard the phrase "the whole is greater than the sum of its parts", I expect. That pretty much captures the essence of an Exton college, at least in its traditional, untainted form. Also a Cambridge college. Probably even small liberal arts colleges in North America. A disparate group of scholars come together, not too many of them, maybe about forty or fifty – all sorts of academic disciplines, people of diverse ages with radically different research interests – and somehow, eventually they form a community where thinking and scholarship can flourish. It's not just that they take meals together, although I must say some of the most interesting seminars I've ever attended have occurred spontaneously over lunch at TH. It's more than that. They govern the college, they look after the students, they listen to each other and provide advice in sometimes the most surprising ways. A biologist, for example, making a comment that opens up a whole new world of enquiry to a sociologist. At least that's how it used to be, before most fellows started calculating their outputs and began to think twice about "donating" their time to activities that wouldn't count. We're still a refuge of sorts from the discipline-based faculties within the University – that's where the main tensions are at present – but only just. And Winston would do his utmost to get some true believer in market forces into the wardenship and turn TH into some sort of money-spinning think tank for government and industry. It would be the end of a noble enterprise, and I'm damned if I'll let it happen, no matter how lame a duck I am!' He smiled at Akiko. 'The juices are flowing again,' he announced, 'but I will spare you the Machiavellian details that are already occurring to me. Now, why don't you tell me what you will be up to in Paris? Fine dining is included, I trust.'

'Of course,' Akiko replied. 'But at the simpler, mid-budget part of the spectrum. I'm just getting together informally with a few colleagues to exchange information about the art market in continental Europe: who's selling what, who's buying what. We do this once a year, with email alerts from time to time in between as necessary. I go to similar meetings every year in New York, Beijing and London. We're particularly interested in new buyers who are spending a lot of money, the "trophy art collectors" we call them, because at least some of them really don't know what they are doing, and that makes them particularly vulnerable to fraud. They have lots of money to spend, much of it newly acquired, and they have houses and condos here and there to "furnish" with impressive paintings and other *objets d'art* that they expect will earn them kudos as connoisseurs. They're prepared to spend a great deal on security for their properties but next to nothing on research into what they're buying, whether it's authentic or indeed legal to acquire. If we identify someone "interesting", we make contact with them via Interpol and offer advice. Confidentially, of course, and no question of fees. Just modest expenses for the advisor involved.'

'Don't the major art auction houses provide the research these people need?' Sir Christopher asked.

'Yes, they do – most of the time,' Akiko replied, 'but they've all made pretty serious errors in determining provenance or authenticity in the not so recent past. Still, it's not them we're really concerned about, or the many reputable dealers we have come to know and trust over the years. It's more the "we can do a package deal" crowd who prey upon these people, offering them instant collections of Etruscan bronzes or *manga* or whatever the collecting fad of the moment happens to be. There's a lot of fake or illegally expropriated Mesopotamian art on sale at the moment, but it's just as likely to be reproduction Chinese antiquities next year.'

'And do you have many takers for the advice you offer?' Sir Christopher asked.

'Not as many as we'd like,' Akiko replied. 'But then – what is the phrase? – you can only lead a horse to water... Still, we've had some successes, and even a few promises of donations to museums from some new collectors. That's what really makes it worthwhile, you know, when these people realize that good art is a treasure, not a commodity.'

'You should ask your colleagues about TKA4,' Sir Christopher said. 'I've heard he's just bought a new villa somewhere in the Emirates and is planning to fill it with contemporary art. I declare an interest, of course, as I would rather he gave a lot more of his money to the College.'

'Where does the Arkwright money come from?' Akiko asked.

'Forestry in Western Canada originally,' Sir Christopher replied, 'or "deforestation" as some of our students prefer to call it, but that was way back in the early 1900s. TKA1 got himself shot dead in 1908, something to do with a logging dispute. TKA2 sold off most of the family's land in the early 1920s, presumably to finance his cross-border bootleg liquor operations during Prohibition in the States, although I gather he kept about 1,000 acres not far from Vancouver. At any rate, he made a lot of money and in 1926 he opted to settle down as a country squire here in South Extonshire, near his father's birthplace in Faringdon, and breed race horses. About as far from his heavily armed rivals as he could get, we figure, and well-timed to avoid both the Wall Street Crash and the repeal of Prohibition a few years later. TKA3 did him proud not only by getting into the University in the early 1930s, but also by marrying the heiress to a significant fortune a few years later. 3 also did some sort of intelligence work during and immediately after the war, and that plus his very generous benefaction to found TH eventually earned him a knighthood. He was what later came to be known as a venture capitalist, and he seems to have been quite adept at zeroing in on promising new opportunities, not only here and in Canada, but also in Asia. When he died a few years ago at the ripe old age of 91, he was said to have been the 500th wealthiest person in Britain.'

'And TKA4?' asked Akiko.

Sir Christopher frowned. 'Not like his father at all. He's more of a deal maker than an entrepreneur, and he couldn't care less about the life of the mind. His father used to love visiting TH, until he suffered a serious stroke two years before he died. He'd attend seminars, have long discussions with fellows about world affairs, meet with students. TKA4 is really only interested in talking to the Bursar about our investment portfolio. He became an ex-pat decades ago to avoid UK taxes and flits from one of his luxurious homes to another, most of them in tax havens, to look after his own investments. Precisely what those are we don't know. Probably property development. He now comes to the UK just once a year for a few months and fits in a brief visit to TH. That suits us just fine, as we can manage to keep him suitably entertained for a day or so. We've learned that he's recently put the Extonshire mansion and surrounding land up for sale at £15 million, so that is focusing our attention on being especially polite and accommodating next week. His father left us a significant bequest, of course, given that he had numerous descendents to provide for as well, but another few millions for the endowment would do no end of good, especially now with the global economy in such a parlous state. You will help us entertain him, won't you? We're having a rather elegant dinner for him on Wednesday night. I will make sure there are some thoroughly engaging people seated nearby.'

'Wednesday night? Hmm, I have a reservation on the flight back to Tokyo late that afternoon,' Akiko said. 'But that can be easily changed, and now that I think of it, I will have some time on Saturday afternoon in Paris to look for something suitable to wear. Who knows, maybe the sales will have started.'

She glanced out the window and saw that the gently rolling countryside had given way to suburbia. They'd be in London soon. She turned her gaze back to Sir Christopher and said, 'Forgive me if you think I'm intruding, but a while back when you were telling me about all the difficulties you've encountered at TH you didn't say anything about your own personal tragedies. Surely those, too, have made life difficult for you.'

Sir Christopher looked startled, and then his face softened. 'Of course,' he said quietly. 'Not so much the divorce. Simone and I hadn't been getting along that well for years, and she really disliked Exton. But losing Lucy, that still hurts. I think of her quite often actually.'

'So does Tom,' Akiko said. 'He's done some sketches of her and a fine watercolour.'

'Tom?' Sir Christopher's face flushed. 'He dashed off to Europe right after her funeral and had a great good time with his mates all summer. I'm not surprised he's been feeling guilty about that. And then leaving Cambridge when he only had one more year to go. Not to mention moving back in with me and playing at being an artist!'

'Chris,' said Akiko, leaning forward. 'Tom *escaped* to Europe. He was in pain, and neither you nor Simone noticed. He got to the hospital long before either of you. They wouldn't let him into Lucy's room because of the fear of contagion, so he had to stand at the window in the corridor and watch her die. It haunts him still that he couldn't do anything for her, comfort her in any way. Of course it was a great shock to you and Simone to lose your daughter. But it was a great shock to Tom, too, to lose his sister.'

Sir Christopher stared at the floor of the compartment. 'It's true Simone was in quite a state when I finally got to the hospital. Her states were really quite extraordinary, I must say. And I was jet-lagged as well as grief-stricken. You're probably right that we paid no attention to Tom. I suppose I should apologize to him for that.'

'Why not just share your thoughts about Lucy, your memories of her?' Akiko asked. 'That's probably more useful now than apologies. And you must see Tom's painting of her. He's quite a good artist.'

'Quite good, you say,' responded Sir Christopher, regaining his composure, 'but is he good enough to make a proper living from it? He'd certainly have more options if he finished his degree.'

'You're probably right about that,' Akiko replied, all too aware of the vagaries of the art world. 'He certainly has good management skills, judging from the way he runs the Lodgings.'

'Runs the Lodgings?' Sir Christopher stood up as the train pulled into Paddington Station. 'Unless I'm mistaken, I'm the Warden of TH and I run the Lodgings as well as the College.'

Akiko stood up, too, 'I'm teasing you, of course,' she said with a smile, 'but surely you must be aware of how much Tom does for you, to earn his keep as it were. The food shopping, the wine deliveries, the dry cleaning, keeping the car in good order and fetching people from airports and train stations. You'd have to get married again to get the same sort of services for such a low cost.'

Sir Christopher picked up Akiko's suitcase and escorted

her to the platform. 'No more marriages for me,' he said as he led her toward the Tube station. 'I rather like being a free agent again. But I take your point about Tom. Maybe I have been treating him a bit like a servant, or a wife as you so delicately put it. I guess I should try to get to know him better.'

'You do that,' Akiko said as they reached the ticket barrier. 'I'll see you on Monday.'

'What time did you say you'll be back?' asked Sir Christopher as he bent down and kissed her on the forehead. 'I'll send Tom...'

Akiko waved a finger at him as she passed through the barrier. 'Talk to Tom instead of sending him on errands,' she called out. 'I might even enjoy the walk from the station if the weather is good. Otherwise I'll take a taxi.' She blew him a kiss and disappeared into the crowd.

CHAPTER 9

'Tom!' Akiko was slightly irritated to see him standing on the platform at Exton Station on Monday afternoon as she stepped down from the train from London. Then she noticed how tense he looked. 'What's wrong?'

'There's been another death,' he replied, taking her suitcase. 'Paula Evans. She worked mornings at TH and did typing and other chores for fellows in various colleges in the afternoons. She was Avery-Hill's secretary.'

As they stood by the car in the near-deserted car park he continued. 'She was cycling along the towpath yesterday afternoon and suddenly she careened into the river. One of the kids playing nearby raised the alarm on his mobile. I'd been having lunch with Sandy, Constable Sanderson, at a pub not far away, so when he got the alert we responded. She'd just been pulled from the water, and the paramedics were trying to resuscitate her. They got some signs of life, but then she went into convulsions and died. I identified her. The police think she'd been poisoned.'

'Poisoned?' Akiko shuddered. 'How awful. What sort of poison?'

'The toxicology report was due earlier this afternoon, according to Sandy. He and Baxter are stopping by at 4.00 to interview Dad and the Bursar, so maybe they'll tell us about it. That's why Dad asked me to come down and fetch you. I had a pretty good idea which train you'd be on.'

They got into the car and headed north through the city centre toward TH. 'By the way,' said Tom, now a bit more relaxed than he'd been previously, 'what magic did you work on Dad?'

'What do you mean?' said Akiko.

'Well,' Tom replied, 'for starters, he *asked* me to fetch you today. But it's more than that. We had a good long chat over breakfast on Saturday. Usually he just buries his face in the newspaper and grumbles about the state of the world.'

'And what was your chat about?' Akiko asked.

'The future,' said Tom. 'His, to begin with, after he finishes as Warden. But mine, too. He didn't badger me to return to Cambridge the way he usually does. He even asked about my paintings. I was going to show him some of them yesterday afternoon, but then this horrible death occurred.'

He turned into the driveway at the Lodgings and parked next to the car that was already there. 'They'll be in the garden, I expect,' he said. 'I'll put your things inside and join you in a minute.'

Sir Christopher rose from the tea table when he saw her and came forward. 'I'm so glad you're back,' he said. 'We're having more trouble, I'm afraid. Did Tom seem all right to you? He was pretty shaken yesterday, having watched that poor woman die.'

'We'll keep an eye on him,' Akiko said reassuringly. Then she greeted Baxter, Sanderson and the Bursar, and sat down. Tom soon arrived and sat down next to her.

Baxter cleared his throat and began. 'One of my colleagues is giving a statement to the local media just about now, informing them that we're treating Mrs Evans's death as unexplained and do not rule out foul play. I'm prepared to be more specific with you, since Tom was there in the company of a police officer and already knows something of our concerns. In our view we are almost certainly dealing with a homicide. The paramedics on the scene suspected something – Mrs Evans didn't respond like a typical drowning victim – and the toxicology report confirms they had grounds for their suspicions. She had high levels of warfarin in her system. That started off as a rat poison, as you probably know, but then it was found to be even more useful in treating people suffering from atrial fibrillation and a few other life-threatening conditions. That's because it decreases blood coagulation and so limits the risk of blood clots in the coronary arteries, lungs or brain. But it requires close monitoring to avoid adverse side effects, and it's very dangerous for unmonitored, not to mention unwitting, users. One dose is unlikely to do much damage, but regular doses over a period of weeks can lead to sudden haemorrhaging and progressive organ failure, precisely what happened in this case. Warfarin is colourless and odourless, so it's easy enough to slip it into someone's food or drink, and there is a lot of it around these days, now that we're all living so much longer. A wonder drug that has saved countless lives, but also a potent means of destroying life.

'It's possible, of course, that Mrs Evans ingested the warfarin herself, either by accident or design. We've spoken to her son, who is her only surviving relative, and he said she had no history of heart trouble or any other condition for which warfarin might have been prescribed. Her GP confirms that. Her son also said she'd been pretty depressed after his step-father's death, but that was five years ago and she'd got back in good spirits fairly soon thereafter. She was planning to retire soon and head off on a round-the-world holiday. Our forensic people report there is no sign of rat infestation at her house in Shillingford and no traces of rodenticides or other poisons on the premises, so there is no basis to question the findings of the toxicology report.

'The Warden and Bursar have been telling me about Mrs Evans's duties here at TH, and we'll start interviewing her friends, neighbours and clients tomorrow. The latter include some of the most illustrious professors in Exton, it turns out, including TH's own Professor Avery-Hill. Apparently he's been taking bed rest since his release from hospital last week, and his wife has insisted we not disturb him. We're checking with his GP and consultant, and I'm sure we'll find a way to interview him soon. We'll also interview some of her close associates here.

'I've already debriefed DC Sanderson, and Tom was interviewed yesterday evening. It's good you both were there so quickly. Sanderson was concentrating on getting statements from witnesses and crowd control, properly enough, but I gather you, Tom, were not that far from the victim when the resuscitation attempts were underway. Is there anything else that has occurred to you about that since yesterday?'

After a brief pause Tom said, 'I was staring down at her from maybe four or five feet away. Her face was turned my way. It was horribly contorted, and I didn't recognize her at first. Then it came to me who she was, and all of a sudden there was a flicker of light in her eyes. At least I think there was. It was as if she'd recognized me, too, and I thought I saw her lips move. Like she was trying to tell me something. No words came out, though, just this deep gurgling sound. She went into convulsions again, and then it was over. She went limp. I watched her features relax until, finally, the paramedics covered her face. It was fascinating the way she returned to looking like her old self once she was dead.'

Sir Christopher stared solemnly into the middle distance. Akiko took Tom's hand and squeezed it gently.

Baxter looked over at Sanderson. 'Do you have anything to add?'

'No, sir,' Sanderson replied, 'except that Social Services have arranged counselling for the youngsters who witnessed the event, if their parents think they need it.'

'Well then, that's it for the moment,' Baxter said as he stood up. 'Except I wonder if I might have a quiet word just now with Ms Sugiyama.'

The others looked slightly surprised but they dutifully stood up and moved away, the Warden and Bursar to the rosery, Tom and Sanderson to the driveway. Baxter sat down again.

'Yes, Inspector?' said Akiko.

'I figure I owe you an apology, Ms Sugiyama,' Baxter said. 'I see now that I misinterpreted the question you asked at our meeting a few days ago in this very same garden. You asked if it made any difference that the police had come to know about the issues that concerned Professor Bates, and I took that to mean simply whether we were going to pursue those issues or leave them to the Warden to resolve. You meant something else, didn't you?'

'It wasn't all that clear in my mind at the time,' Akiko replied quietly, 'and no doubt I didn't express myself as well as I should have. But I was reminded of what I felt then when Tom met me at the station today and told me the latest awful news. It's just that I couldn't make sense of what Professor Bates had done. That he had stopped taking his medication was one thing – my own father did that not long ago, having decided his time to die had come. No, it was the staging of it all, the elaborate steps he took to make sure Professor Avery-Hill's misdeeds became as widely known as possible. There was such passion in that. Such apparently noble passion.'

'Bates as martyr to the cause of traditional academic values?' Baxter asked.

'Precisely,' said Akiko. 'Of course, I have no doubt he cared greatly about those values, about intellectual integrity, scholarship, teaching. But is that enough to account for what he did? For his hatred of Avery-Hill?'

'I see we share a similar view of human nature, Ms Sugiyama,' Baxter observed. 'In my profession, it's usually enough just to find one motive and link that up with opportunity: hey presto, crime solved. But there certainly are layers of motivation in just about everything we do, whether criminal or not. What other layers do you think we're dealing with here?'

'I don't know enough about England to say,' Akiko replied. 'But if this had happened in Japan I'd be pretty sure there were personal motivations involved, in addition to the principles. Not just in what Bates did, but in the outcome, too. Maybe you should do some deeper background checks on the people concerned.'

'So you think there is some sort of a connection between his death and the death of Mrs Evans?' Baxter asked.

'Don't you?' Akiko asked in reply. 'Aren't you a bit concerned about what might happen next?'

Baxter looked at her intently. 'Just between the two of us,

yes, I am concerned. That's the main reason why I wanted to talk to you. There's been a lot of tension brewing within the University for years. It could well get worse. You notice things, Ms Sugiyama, you read people well, and I hope you'll contact me if anything else occurs to you while you're here. England is probably not that different from Japan, in the final analysis.'

'Please call me Akiko,' Akiko said. 'Everyone does, and I like it. Have you ever been to Japan?'

Baxter fumbled in his jacket pocket and produced a card, which he handed to her. 'Here are my contact numbers,' he said, 'in case you need to get in touch, Akiko. I'm James. And no, I've never been to Japan. But I do like sushi.'

'That's promising,' Akiko said, slipping the card into her purse. 'I'm sure we'll meet again, James, before I head home. Of course, I will address you as Inspector when circumstances so require.'

'And when are you heading home?' Baxter asked.

'It was to have been the day after tomorrow,' Akiko replied, 'but the Warden asked me to stay on a day longer, to help him entertain the TH benefactor on Wednesday night, and then I found out that my airline was fully booked up until Sunday.'

'So maybe we might get together for dinner at some point?' asked Baxter. 'To discuss developments in the case, off the record as it were.'

'To discuss developments in the case.' Akiko mimicked his serious tone.

Baxter looked distinctly uncomfortable. 'It's just that, well, I admire the way your mind works.'

'The way my mind works,' she said flatly.

Baxter shook his head wearily and then grinned across

the table at her. 'This was a lot easier when I was younger,' he said, 'or so I vaguely remember. Right, then. A fresh start. I like the way you look and the way you frown just a bit when you're thinking. You intrigue me in all sorts of ways, and I want to get to know you better. How about dinner tomorrow night, say around 7.30?'

'I'd be delighted,' Akiko replied brightly. 'I'd like to get to know you better, too. But right now we need to be aware that the Warden is approaching. Shall we make some business-like farewells?'

Baxter stood up and took Akiko's outstretched hand in his. 'Very helpful,' he said. 'Thank you so much.' He ran his thumb lightly along her fingers. 'I'll see you tomorrow then. Ah, Warden. My apologies for banishing you from your own tea table, but Ms Sugiyama has just given me some very useful insight into a famous poisoning case in Japan. I figured it was best not to upset the others with the details.'

'I'm happy to have been of assistance, Inspector,' said Akiko. She smiled warmly at both men and headed toward the Lodgings.

CHAPTER 10

'A date? With DCI Baxter?' Sir Christopher sat in the armchair in the library, nursing a brandy. Akiko sat at his desk, gently rubbing the excess glue from the outer surface of the vase with one of the finely grained polishing cloths she had brought with her from Japan. She had been at it for just over an hour, and the end was almost in sight. It was a little past 10.00 on Monday night.

'I said dinner, not a "date"', Akiko protested, 'and I only mentioned it so that you could make plans for tomorrow without having to worry about entertaining me. Why is it that when a man and a woman meet up for a meal, people immediately think something's going on? And what do you have against Baxter? Surely you don't think he's inferior to your own sort here in Exton?'

'Of course not!' replied Sir Christopher. 'I have many shortcomings, but snobbery is not one of them. Baxter is smart, he's very good at his job, not bad looking either in a weathered sort of way. But he is weathered, you know. He must be in his mid-fifties.'

Akiko gently put down the vase, pushed her chair back a safe distance and burst into laughter.

Sir Christopher was so startled he almost dropped his brandy snifter. 'What's so funny?' he asked.

'*You* are so funny,' said Akiko, once she'd caught her breath.

'You're treating me like some naïve teenager. Do you have any idea how old I am?' she asked.

'Well, no,' he muttered. 'I've been brought up not to calculate ladies' ages. Let's see, we first met in Lyon in the early 1980s, didn't we? You were quite young then…'

'I was twenty-four, and that was almost three decades ago, Chris. I'm fifty-two now. I'm practically as old as Baxter, assuming you're right about his age.'

'But you're not in the least bit weathered,' Sir Christopher said defensively. 'Sorry, that doesn't sound like much of a compliment, does it. What I mean is you look as lovely as ever you did. All right, I'm sorry, too, about my response to your news about dinner. Too much wardening, I suspect. It seems I am forever consoling the young who have loved unwisely. At any rate, I accept that Baxter is not a cradle robber, and besides, I know you are thoroughly capable of looking after yourself.'

'Apology accepted,' said Akiko as she returned to the desk and resumed sanding. 'Many thanks for the compliments, too.'

'Are you sure you won't join me in a brandy?' Sir Christopher asked.

'I think I need another five minutes or so on this vase,' she replied, 'but yes, then a brandy would be great.'

Sir Christopher headed off to the kitchen, checked his email on the laptop he kept there and returned to the library just as Akiko was dusting the vase with another cloth. She turned the vase carefully under one of the lamps. 'Done!' she announced.

'And here is your reward, my dear,' said Sir Christopher, handing her a snifter. He settled back into his chair, and

Akiko relaxed into hers. 'It was so good of you to respond to my distress call last week and attend to this vase,' he said. 'And I'm even more grateful for your advice about Tom. He and I had a good conversation the other day, the first in years.'

'So Tom told me on the way back from the station,' said Akiko, swirling the brandy gently in her snifter. 'Hmm, this is lovely,' she murmured after taking a sip. 'To you and Tom!' she said, raising her glass. 'And to you, my dear old friend, Sir Chris. You've helped me out on more than one occasion, so I was more than happy to come to your rescue.'

Sir Christopher chuckled. 'You *were* a bit of a "naïve teenager" during your time in France, as I now recall. And I've enjoyed the little assignments you've given me over the years since. A discreet phone call here, checking out an art gallery there. It was most satisfying to see those forgers in Amiens put out of business.'

He was silent for a moment and then said gently, 'I was truly sorry to hear your news about Peter last year.'

'It was so sudden,' Akiko said with a slight shudder. 'He'd had job offers in the States before, but he'd always turned them down. Then one day he just announced that he'd had an offer from the Getty that was simply too good to refuse. "Besides," he said, "it's time I went home." That was it. As if the twelve years we'd spent together in Tokyo were just some sort of interval in his real life. He packed up and was gone. I felt so numb. Then I got angry, and then my father became terminally ill. So I too went home. It was therapeutic in a strange sort of way, looking after him, getting to know him again, seeing a lot of my childhood friends. I eventually stopped thinking about Peter.'

She emptied her glass, as did the Warden. 'I'll fish out a spare key for you in the morning,' he said. 'That way I won't be tempted to wait up until you are safely back tomorrow night. I think I can put my wardening instincts on hold in your case. Enjoy yourself!'

Akiko grinned. She gave him a big hug and made her way upstairs.

CHAPTER 11

Tuesday had definitely been the best day of her recent trip to Exton, Akiko reflected when she was back in Tokyo. With Tom's help, she had prepared the enamels first thing in the morning, and she'd finished the painting on the vase well before noon. She'd been rather pleased with her handiwork. There were a few imperfections, to be sure, but they were mostly on one facet. Careful placement in the display case would take care of that. They had closed the curtains in the library, cleaned the brushes and gone off to a leisurely lunch at Tom's favourite pub. Then taken a walk on the sun-drenched river bank. Tom had told her he was making enquiries about returning to Cambridge in October. 'I can focus on art history,' he'd said. 'The tripos system there allows for a major shift in field of study for the final year, unlike here in Exton, so it might actually be interesting. Much more interesting than the history and theory of literary criticism, at any rate.'

But the highlight of the day had been dinner with James. Both the Warden and Tom had disappeared from the Lodgings at supper time, she remembered with a wry smile, so she was on her own when he had arrived, hardly a minute past 7.30. They'd driven to an Italian restaurant in the little market town of Oxford, to the north of Exton, eaten extremely well and laughed a lot as they shared Interpol stories. He did look so handsome when he laughed. 'Will you come over to my place for a while?' he'd asked when they got back to his car, and she'd readily agreed. He'd made coffee, they'd talked a bit about themselves and then as if it was the most natural thing for them to do they'd made love. He had such expressive eyes, such gentle hands. If only he wasn't now 6,000 miles away, Akiko thought to herself, he'd be perfect. But then, he was coming to visit her for two weeks in late September. 'I'll make sure you get some proper sushi,' she'd written in a recent email. 'That's not why I'm coming to Tokyo,' he'd replied. Down-to-Basics Baxter indeed, she thought happily.

Wednesday, by contrast, had been a long and ultimately hard day. Akiko and Tom got the vase into the display case in the SCR a little after 10.00 and re-arranged some nearby chairs and standard lamps so that the case occupied pride of place in its corner of the room. After a celebratory coffee in the Buttery Tom headed back to the Lodgings and Akiko went to the Warden's office to keep him company while he waited for TKA4. His secretary finally buzzed him at 12.40. 'Arriving at 4.00,' she reported. 'His new P.A. seems a lot more efficient than the last one, and no, she won't be coming with him. I'll amend the seating plan for dinner.'

Sir Christopher thanked her and smiled at Akiko. 'We're spared until teatime,' he said. 'Now we can really enjoy the lunch the Chef has prepared "just in case".'

They made their way to a private room adjacent to the Fellows' Dining Room, where the Bursar and the Senior Tutor, Dr Susan McKenzie, were already present. Akiko noted that both of them relaxed when told TKA4 would not be joining them. The Steward deftly removed the fifth place setting while they sipped their glasses of sherry.

'Did you see the item about Rupert Caldwell in this morning's FT?' the Bursar asked as they sat down to a first course of watercress soup.

'David, you know I'm not numerate enough to understand the *Financial Times*,' Sir Christopher replied. 'What is our wealthiest former student up to now?'

'He's just sold his little biotech company for £230 million,' the Bursar said with a grin. 'Apparently he wants to focus more of his time and money on renewable energy projects. Perhaps we should invite him back to TH in the fall.'

'Yes, I agree,' Sir Christopher said. 'It does seem an appropriate moment. Maybe to give a talk to some of our students, followed by dinner, of course, and some gentle persuasion about how he might make significant contributions to the future of the College. But the University Development Office will be interested in him, too. Can you make a deal with them to give us first crack at him?'

'I can try,' the Bursar said. 'But it will be harder to keep Boris and the other science fellows here from trying to interest him in their pet projects. You'll need to bring them on side.'

Sir Christopher looked apologetically at Akiko as the soup dishes were cleared away and the main course of pan-fried sea bass, mange-touts and new potatoes served. 'Ah, Akiko my dear. Yet another dark side of Exton life is revealed to you. But without benefactors we would be in a sorry state indeed.'

'Is there no TKA5?' Akiko asked, savouring the perfectly cooked fish.

Susan McKenzie laughed. 'Oh yes there is,' she said, 'but he is a prodigal son if ever there was one. Name your stereotype – fast cars, women, wine – and he measures up.

Worse yet, he attended university in the States and his alma mater is doing all it can to get its hands on some of his money. We figure we must diversify our fund-raising beyond the Arkwright family, but unfortunately we still don't have many seriously wealthy former students. What's the tally now, David?'

'Precisely three, with the other two way behind Caldwell,' the Bursar replied glumly. He turned to Akiko and said, 'We're a graduate college, you see, and most of our students have ended up in academic or public sector careers here and abroad. Good for academe and the public sector, but not at all promising for our endowment.'

Sir Christopher sighed as he took a final bite of new potato. 'Do you suppose TKA4 will agree to the bursary fund we're proposing, Susan? God knows our students need all the help they can get with fees and thesis research costs now that other sources are drying up apace.'

'David and I have put all the relevant documentation into one tidy package, priced at £1.2 million,' the Senior Tutor replied. 'The safe take on that would be about £40,000 per year, just barely enough for a useful range and number of grants. We sent him a copy of the proposal last week, and we'll review it with him later today. We've got the post-doc his father endowed as a precedent, and of course he can name the fund as he wishes, so I am reasonably hopeful.'

'He also knows we got £5 million from his father's estate just four years ago,' the Bursar added, 'so he's likely to have been thinking he's off the hook for a while longer. That's why we included a page on how income from the endowment has been spent in recent years. What with employment and building maintenance costs, we barely get by, especially now that our income has been battered by the recent economic downturn. I'm a bit more pessimistic than Susan, but I do hope that TKA4's ego will come to our rescue. He's been basking in his role as benefactor of "his favourite Exton college" for some time now and is aware he needs to prove himself a worthy successor to his father. That said, we may well have some hard bargaining ahead.'

Over lemon sorbet, their conversation turned to plans for the afternoon and evening ahead. Tea in the Warden's office to start, at which Susan and David would review their proposal, then an hour for TKA4 to meet privately with the Bursar to share investment strategies. The Warden would collect TKA4 at 6.00, give him a leisurely tour of the grounds and take him to the Lodgings for further lobbying on the bursaries front. Drinks in the SCR at 7.00 with Akiko and the fifteen fellows who had been mustered for the occasion, and dinner at 7.30. With any luck TKA4 would be in his car and away by 10.30, and TH just might be in a position to do more for its students.

* * *

'I have a better idea,' TKA4 announced after the review of the bursary proposal. 'You're asking for funds to do the same old thing, help produce yet more people with doctorates who are fit only for careers as academics. Why don't we shake things up a bit? Give these bright youngsters some idea of the alternatives open to them. Okay, let them do a Master's degree, but after that they have to do a one-year work placement out in the real world of business and industry. That's what was recommended at a seminar sponsored by the Department for

Business, Innovation and Skills I attended a few weeks ago. Get some good young minds plugged into doing their best for the UK economy, and let employers have a chance to offer the best among them permanent jobs. Even those students the employers are not interested in and who have no choice but to go back to university for their doctorates would have a better idea of how they could interact with business and industry in future. You know, how to communicate with wealth creators, the sort of research projects they could undertake that would be really useful to this country.'

'I see,' said the Warden. 'An intriguing concept to be sure. It might be of interest to some of our students in science and engineering, but I'm less sure about those in other fields. What do you think, Susan?'

'Well, yes,' the Senior Tutor replied, 'I agree it's an intriguing concept and maybe some of the students in the social sciences would be interested, too. But roughly one-third of our students are working on degrees in the humanities, and some of their research interests don't mesh easily with those of the corporate world.'

'Precisely!' TKA4 said. 'That's one of the things the officials at BIS are particularly concerned about. Who needs more studies of the classics or poetry? Or even Shakespeare, valuable though he is to the tourism industry? Universities need to rethink their degree programmes, make them more relevant to the 21st century. And maybe a work placement at, say, the BBC or the *Times* would make some of your young humanities students change direction, too. They'd earn a lot more money working for the media than they'd ever make as academics.'

'No doubt you're right about that,' the Senior Tutor replied, 'but we also have the problem of completion rates for graduate students, no matter what their fields. The various funding councils that provide tuition and maintenance grants to the most promising UK graduate students expect them to complete their doctoral degrees within four consecutive years, and universities are penalized if delays occur. So some of our best students wouldn't be able to apply for work placements. I expect the greatest interest would be among self-funded overseas students, but most of them do eventually return to their home countries. So it's likely to be other economies that benefit.'

TKA4 looked a bit puzzled. 'Well, that didn't come up at the seminar,' he said after a pause, 'but given that BIS now controls higher education policy in this country I'm sure such a little wrinkle can be ironed out in no time.'

'And you would contribute to this initiative in some way?' the Bursar asked.

'Of course,' said TKA4. 'Unfortunately not to the extent you propose. I'm still coping with death duties on my father's estate, but once the Extonshire house is sold I figure I can hand over a cheque for, say, £500,000. That would be to endow some bursaries for students on Master's degree courses. BIS officials will coordinate the work placement scheme and, of course, the companies offering the placements will provide the students selected with basic salaries for the year. Very basic probably, but still higher than their maintenance grants.'

'You couldn't contribute anything to help our PhD students?' the Senior Tutor asked.

TKA4 shrugged his shoulders. 'Not at the moment, I'm afraid. Maybe if I can find a buyer for some Japanese art I've inherited. I certainly have no desire to keep it, but the estimate

I've received is not that promising. Maybe another £150,000?'

'That would certainly be helpful,' the Warden said as he stood up to bring the meeting to an end, 'and the funding you propose for our Master's degree students is most welcome. We remain indebted to the Arkwright family and look forward to expressing our appreciation this evening. For the moment, however, I know you and David have matters to discuss. As always we do appreciate your advice on our investment strategy.'

After handshakes all around, TKA4 and the Bursar left the room. The Warden and Senior Tutor slumped back into their chairs.

'That was excruciatingly painful,' Susan said a minute later, once she was sure their benefactor was out of earshot.

'I agree,' Sir Christopher replied. 'What will BIS do to us next? They keep moving the goalposts, HEFCE has to follow suit and we're left to pick up the pieces. I'll do my best to talk up doctoral degrees when I see TKA4 later, but I guess our best hope is that he gets a better price for his father's Japanese art collection. Hmm, you haven't met her yet, Susan, but I have a visitor who knows a lot about Japanese art, and she's joining us at dinner tonight. Maybe she can help.'

* * *

Akiko had spent the afternoon in the city centre buying souvenirs for other members of the Art Squad and two of her neighbours. She was particularly pleased with the specialty teas she had found for her staff, as they wouldn't weigh down her luggage, but she had indulged in three heavy jars of the fine-cut Exton marmalade she had enjoyed so much at breakfast at the Lodgings. One each for Mrs Nakamura and Mrs Ishida, who looked after the plants on her balcony and collected her mail whenever she was away, and one for her. She'd walked back to TH a little after 5.00 and was about to take a shower when the phone rang. There was no one else in the house at the time, and after several rings she decided to answer it.

'The Warden's Lodgings,' she said in what she thought was an appropriately official tone of voice, while reaching for the pen and paper on her bedside table so she could take down a message.

'I was hoping it would be you who answered,' Baxter said. 'I've got to be at a meeting in minutes, but I just wanted to say, um, well I don't know exactly what I want to say. Is everything okay with you?'

'Very okay, more than okay in fact,' Akiko replied. 'Are we still on for tomorrow evening?'

'Yes we are, of course we are,' said Baxter. 'Look, I've got to go now, but I am really looking forward to seeing you again. Well, best of luck with that fund-raising dinner at TH tonight.'

'Oh, I'll be on the fringes of all that, James,' Akiko said. 'Just another woman at the dining table, I expect. I promised to be there but I'd rather be with you.'

Baxter paused briefly before replying. 'So we'll have some catching up to do,' he said. 'I'll do my best to make the wait worthwhile.'

Akiko laughed. 'You've already done pretty well as far as I'm concerned,' she said. 'Just more of the same, please.'

'Right then. Lots more of the same. Goodbye for now, Akiko.'

'Goodbye, James,' Akiko said. She put the phone back in

the receiver and fell back on the bed, smiling. Then she noticed the time and dashed to the bathroom.

* * *

Sir Christopher and TKA4 were standing by the fireplace in the living room of the Lodgings when Akiko came downstairs at 6.45. She was wearing the jade-green silk trouser suit she had bought in Paris, and she noted with satisfaction that both men seemed impressed by her appearance.

'I am very pleased to meet you, Mr Arkwright,' she said as introductions were made. 'Sir Christopher has told me so much about you and your family.'

'And he's just told me you're an expert on Japanese art,' TKA4 replied with typical directness. 'Will you come to my country house tomorrow afternoon and give me your assessment of my father's collection?'

Akiko glanced at the Warden, relieved that he'd not been referring to the vase but unsure about this new call on her expertise. Sir Christopher smiled back benignly and explained that proceeds from the sale of the collection would benefit TH. TKA4 added that many of the items were 'small' or 'pale', not at all to his taste, so he was happy to see them go. She didn't like his dismissal of the delicacy she prized so highly in her country's artistic heritage, but she forced herself to smile back at him.

'I'm hardly an expert on current valuations,' she said, 'but I do know people in this country who are. And I have some idea of what museums and private collectors are really interested in these days. So I might be able to give you some useful advice.'

'Excellent!' TKA4 said. 'I'll expect you and Chris at 3.00. Now, isn't it time for drinks and dinner? I'm thirsty as well as famished.'

Sir Christopher took Akiko's arm as they made their way to the SCR. 'Thank you, my dear,' he whispered. 'By the way, you look smashing.'

'Thank you, Chris. On sale, as I had hoped,' she whispered back.

'Do you mind if I ask Tom to drive us tomorrow?' he asked. 'I tend to get lost on country roads.'

'Not very promising for your rural idyll, is it?' Akiko replied. 'But okay, so long as you ask him.'

* * *

Akiko was seated to TKA4's right at dinner, but as promised there was more congenial company nearby. She thoroughly enjoyed talking to Dr Kim on her right about the latest Korean soap operas to top the viewing charts in Japan and to Professor Brady opposite her at table about French politics. After the main course of roast saddle of lamb had been served she dutifully turned to TKA4.

'It must be a bit wrenching to part with your familial home,' she said.

TKA4 shrugged his shoulders. 'Not really,' he replied. 'I only lived there until I was seven and then I was sent away to boarding school. Besides, the place costs a fortune to maintain. No, I much prefer life at my houses in the Caymans and Gstaad, and I've just bought an exquisite villa in Dubai. I'm in touch with an agency about decorating it with big, bold pieces of contemporary art.'

Akiko looked at him intently. 'I see,' she said. 'Which artists interest you?'

'Oh, I'm leaving all that to the agency,' TKA4 said. 'They have the floor plans and an excellent track record in selecting the works of younger artists that will appreciate in value very quickly. I've given them a budget of £200,000, and they say the collection should be worth at least twice that within five years.'

'How interesting,' Akiko replied, hoping that he didn't notice her slight shudder. 'And how wonderful to be able to spend time in Dubai. I only spent a weekend there about five years ago, but I found it fascinating. The daylight was so crystal clear, so pure. And the sea so inviting! Such beautiful carpets in the shops, too.'

'Well, we'll have our own swimming pool and my wife prefers white wall-to-wall carpeting, so we won't be going native,' TKA4 said as the Steward refilled his wine glass. 'Now tell me, Ms Sugiyama, when is that country of yours going to start growing again?'

Akiko smiled back at him. 'I haven't the faintest idea, I'm afraid,' she said. 'What do you think?' She then had to listen to his long disquisition on global economic realities and the continuing power of market forces until, finally, she was rescued by the dessert course and able to strike up a conversation with Dr Kim again.

Ten minutes later the Warden stood up and made an elegant after-dinner speech charting the history of Arkwright munificence to TH and praising TKA4 for his continuing support. There was prolonged applause when he finished and then everyone repaired to the SCR for coffee and brandy. Akiko stood on the far side of the room, opposite the display case, and noticed that hardly anyone paid any attention to it or its contents. Adele Williamson eventually came and joined her.

'Hi,' she said. 'I'm Adele, one of the fellows here, and you must be the Warden's guest, Ms Sugiyama. I was here the night the vase got broken, and I gather we have you to thank for putting it back together again. It looks great.'

'Why thank you,' Akiko said. 'Do call me Akiko. Sir Christopher had told me it is almost impossible to keep a secret in an Exton college, but I was beginning to wonder about that.'

'I won't bore you with the sociological evidence,' Adele said, 'but there are secrets to be shared and secrets to keep. We at TH have plenty of them to keep these days, mostly about our impact strategies, so it's been refreshing to have one we feel it is safe to talk about.'

'Yes, I've noticed the same thing about secrets in my own work,' Akiko replied, 'and I gather things are pretty tough here with the new appraisal scheme looming. I have to file an annual performance report to my trustees, of course, but they leave me and my team pretty much alone to deal with our work as we see fit.'

'As used to be the case for us,' Adele said with a sigh, 'before we got hit by all these reforms. I do wish the government would regulate banks more and us less.'

Just then Sir Christopher came up to them and announced that TKA4 was heading home. 'Fortunately he has a driver,' he said sotto voce. 'Come, let's see him off.'

CHAPTER 12

It was 8.45 on Thursday morning. Akiko was at the laptop in the kitchen, responding to emails from her office in Tokyo. Sir Christopher, seated at the kitchen table, had just finished reading his newspapers.

'Tom and I are going to the cinema this evening,' he said. 'Apparently there's a film showing that he says I simply must see. Some sort of comedy about the miseries and pitfalls of country life. Would you care to join us? It might help us all recover from our outing to Arkwright Manor this afternoon.'

Akiko turned to look at him. 'I have a date with James tonight. He's picking me up around 9.30.'

'That's an intriguingly late hour for a date, at least for mature folk such as you and me,' responded Sir Christopher. 'Do I take it that "something's going on"? Hmm, yes, I see it does, as you're blushing just a bit. Quite attractively so, I hasten to add.'

'He's fifty-six,' Akiko said, returning his smile. 'Divorced for years, has two grown children and one granddaughter, Sophie, who'll be four years old this Sunday. And yes, there's something going on. I like him a lot, Chris. He's rather complicated, but then so am I. And I do love puzzles!'

'So should I fetch a key for you for tonight? No, I can see not, as you're blushing attractively again. But, that said, I'll get you a key anyway, in case there's no-one at home in the morning. Keep it as long as you like.'

Just then the doorbell rang, and Sir Christopher got up to answer it. Baxter, holding a thick manila envelope in one hand, stood on the doorstep. 'Do come in, Inspector,' Sir Christopher said warmly. 'I was just heading off to my office, but I expect it is really Akiko you want to see. She's in the kitchen keeping Art Watch East going via the Internet.'

'Good morning, Warden,' said Baxter, slightly startled by the warmth of his greeting. 'And yes, I did come to see Ms Sugiyama. I'm hoping she will give me her opinion of some data we've collected at her suggestion. It might well prove helpful in our ongoing investigation.'

'Of course,' Sir Christopher replied. 'And now if you'll excuse me, I'll just head off to my work while you head off to yours. The kitchen is over to your right.' He stepped out the front door and closed it behind him.

Akiko appeared in the entry hall. 'I heard your voice,' she said.

'I think the Warden knows about us,' Baxter said as he embraced her.

'And I admire the way your mind works,' replied Akiko, returning his kisses.

Baxter laughed as he released her. 'I missed you yesterday, all day and all night,' he said gently, 'but I'm afraid I've come to see you on business this morning. We've made some progress on the background checks you suggested the other day, and I thought maybe you'd take a look at our findings?'

'Of course,' replied Akiko.

They sat down next to one another at the dining room table, and Baxter took a sheaf of papers from the envelope he was carrying. 'I can't show you the results of the criminal records sweeps we did, or sweeps of a few other confidential databases, but I can tell you that absolutely nothing significant turned up. What I have here our researcher has gleaned from *Who's Who* and a few other public sources. Not only about Bates and Avery-Hill, but also everyone else on Mrs Evans's client list. Thirteen people in all: her twelve clients, plus Bates. Here's the summary table she just faxed me this morning: each name, current address, place and date of birth, educational history, employment history and any honours or awards.'

'Hmm,' said Akiko, scanning the table. 'I can't make much sense of all these birthplaces, but I see Bates and Avery-Hill went to the same secondary school.'

'Yes, Manchester Grammar,' said Baxter. 'They were a year apart. But they went to different universities, Bates to Exton and Avery-Hill to the LSE. I didn't expect you to be intimately familiar with the geography of Britain, so I cobbled this crude map together last night. All the birthplaces are marked with the relevant initials. And so are the schools and universities these people attended. The birthplaces are pretty widely spread, but there's a definite clustering on the latter two variables, especially universities. That's only to be expected. After all, these men are now in their mid-to late sixties, if not even older, and given that they've made it to the top of the academic profession, as it were, that means they were bright enough to have soared through all the ranks of the elite educational system that still prevailed in the 1950s and 60s. There were far fewer universities and university places back then – maybe enough places for about 10 per cent of the age cohort – and there was a relatively small number of schools that prepared their pupils for successful entrance to those universities.'

'What did you say just now?' Akiko asked.

'About university entrance?'

'No, before that, about their ages?'

'I said the people we're considering are all in their mid-to late sixties, if not even older,' Baxter answered in a puzzled tone.

'No, you said "men", didn't you?' Akiko said. 'Where are the women? Bates was a bachelor as I recall, but Avery-Hill has a wife, doesn't he? Aren't any of these other men married? Do you have any information on that?'

'For that you have to look at the top of each entry in the *Who's Who*,' said Baxter. He reached for a stack of photocopies and slid the first page toward her. 'Under "m" for "married to", as just here. It's the wife's maiden name that's given, of course. Ah, I see. If we can find out where the wives came from and what their fathers did for a living, we could well find some connections there. Young women were nowhere near as mobile back in the 70s as they are nowadays.'

Akiko smiled at him. 'It can get pretty personal between a man and a woman,' she said.

'I've been reminded of that recently,' said Baxter, smiling back at her. 'I'm certainly looking forward to getting personal with you again tonight.'

'And, of course, things can go wrong,' Akiko continued. 'In fact, they quite often do. Some people can get over their losses, and some cannot. People can do strange, sometimes violent things when they're disappointed in love.'

'Or because they want to protect a loved one,' Baxter added. 'Excuse me just a minute,' he murmured as he reached for his mobile. 'Good morning, Janet,' he said after a brief interval. 'I don't suppose Stella is around? I see. Well, leave her a note or, better yet, send her an email. Tell her to make up a report on the wives of Mrs Evans's clients, starting with the *Who's Who* entries. Place of birth essential. She might need access to some non-public records for that. School and university records would be helpful, too. Also whatever information she can find on their fathers' occupations.' He stroked the back of Akiko's neck lightly as he spoke. 'She'll know where to look. Have her check out Bates's father, too. If she can't get started until this afternoon, she can fax me in the morning.'

He switched off his phone and turned to Akiko. 'Some sort of child care crisis. She probably won't be in until late this afternoon. But she's very good, Exton trained of course, and now that there are so many records available to the police online, it's almost easier for her to work at home into the wee hours. Thanks for that nudge. It could prove interesting.'

'You're welcome, James,' Akiko replied. 'I'm looking forward to tonight, too.'

Baxter leaned over and kissed her. 'I'm glad to hear that,' he whispered in her ear, 'because I spent a good hour last night cleaning my flat.'

Akiko laughed and sat back. 'So how is the case going?' she asked.

Baxter reached for another paper. 'We're just about finished with the interviews,' he said. 'We spoke to her neighbours and close associates here at TH on Tuesday. We finally got to see Avery-Hill yesterday afternoon, but I left that to one of my colleagues. I am not at the moment one of his favourite representatives of Thames Valley Police, after all. My colleague also interviewed three of Mrs Evans's other clients. I saw five of them yesterday, and I have three more to see today, one in

Aldworth and the other two in North Exton. We're having a case meeting at 4.00. That should be over by 6.00, but then I have to make an appearance at Town Hall at 7.00 to discuss crime management in Extonshire with a group of concerned residents. The Chief Constable will be there, too, so maybe I can slip away a bit earlier and come for you before 9.30.'

'And do you know if Mrs Evans visited any of her clients at their home recently?' Akiko asked. 'Where had she been on Sunday, I wonder?'

Baxter looked at her admiringly. 'Your mind is working in a particularly intriguing fashion this morning, my dear Akiko,' he said. 'We've examined her diary, of course. Fortunately, it had been in her handbag inside her knapsack and so didn't get too wet. The entries just give initials and times, not places. Why should they, after all. She knew where all her clients were. "A-H" is noted down for both Friday and Sunday, and we know he was staying at home then. Three of the people I've already interviewed stated she always came to their homes, usually on a weekly basis, including last week. They are all retired and no longer have college rooms. She saw the others in their colleges, except I suppose when urgent deadlines loomed. I'll be sure to ask the clients I see today. Speaking of which, I've got to go now, I regret to say. It's almost 9.30 and I'm due in some remote corner of the countryside at 10.00.'

He gathered up the papers and returned them to the envelope.

'I don't suppose you know how many of these people are taking warfarin?' Akiko asked as she accompanied him to the door.

'There are limits to police powers in this country, I am

usually glad to say,' Baxter replied. 'We can't just go barging into GP surgeries or chemists demanding that kind of information, not without just cause and the proper warrants. But don't worry, we coppers can be very sympathetic interviewers, as and when necessary, and most people are far more willing to talk about their own troubles than those of others when given half a chance.'

'And what did her clients think about Mrs Evans herself?' Akiko asked at the doorway.

'Now that's a very interesting question,' Baxter replied as he stepped outside. 'Most of the people I saw spoke very warmly of her, but one seemed a bit negative about her. I'll be sure to bring that up at the case meeting.' He glanced at his watch. 'I'm running late,' he said as he embraced her. 'I should forewarn you that I'll be in uniform when I come to get you tonight,' he added. 'It reassures the local public that they're being looked after properly, we're told.'

'How very interesting,' said Akiko as she stood on tiptoe to kiss him. 'Like many Japanese I am still wary of men in uniform. But it's okay. I doubt you'll keep yours on for long.'

Baxter chuckled. 'Another brilliant deduction, my dear Akiko.' He stroked her cheek, kissed her on her forehead and headed for his car.

CHAPTER 13

Baxter picked up Sanderson outside the Exton Playhouse, as they'd agreed the previous evening, and headed for Station Road. 'Sorry to be late,' he said. 'Have you been waiting long?'

'Only about five minutes,' the constable replied. 'It took me longer than I'd thought to find a space for my car at the Northern Park & Ride, and I just missed a bus. Commuting into Exton city centre every day must be a nightmare.'

'I expect it is,' said Baxter. 'We're lucky to be based in a lower-cost district where most of us can still afford to live. Not like these professors we're interviewing who came to the University decades ago when housing in Exton was still relatively cheap.'

The road to the south of the city centre was jammed with bicycles, cars and buses, but once they got through the bottleneck at the rail station they made good time on the virtually empty southbound lane of the A329, and in less than fifteen minutes they made the turn to Aldworth. Baxter followed Sanderson's instructions and turned onto a narrow lane just past the village shop. At the end of it stood a large stone house, set in extensive grounds.

As Baxter and Sanderson approached the door it was opened by a man with thick glasses and long white hair. 'Hello!' he called out warmly. 'Do come in. I'm Andrew

Collins, and I figure you must be the police. My wife has made us coffee.'

Professor Collins, author of some dozen books in philosophy, ushered them into the living room, where his wife Estelle sat next to a table laden with cake as well as coffee. She stood up carefully after introductions were made and started serving refreshments. 'It's so very tragic about Paula,' she said. 'She was a good friend as well an excellent secretary for Andrew. It's been rather lonely here since the children grew up and moved away.'

Baxter, figuring that 'the children' must have grown up and moved away at least thirty years ago, smiled at both of them and settled into the chair to which he had been directed, and Sanderson sat down, too. 'It's very kind of you to help us with our enquires,' Baxter said, 'and I do apologize for being a bit late for our appointment. Of course, we share your sadness over the death of Mrs Evans, and anything you can tell us about her – the work she did for you, her friendship – may well prove helpful.'

'I've always done my serious writing in longhand,' Professor Collins said. 'Some say it's just a schoolboy habit, but I find it suits the way my mind works. I have a computer, of course, which is fine for email and memos, but there's nothing like a blank sheet of lined paper to get me thinking, and there's a sort of synergy between my brain and my hand. Or maybe it's the pen in my hand, inviting me to write more and waiting patiently until I do so.'

'But then someone has to type up the results,' his wife interjected. 'I used to do that, until my arthritis made it impossible. That's when Paula came to the rescue. About four years ago, wasn't it?'

'Yes,' replied Professor Collins, 'just a year or so before I retired. She came to my workroom in All Saints' once a week, and then she started coming out here by car. I paid her extra to cover the cost of petrol. She was very efficient.'

'And so helpful,' his wife added. 'She'd always phone beforehand to see if we needed anything from the shops. And she'd sit with me and fill me in on all the latest college gossip while Andrew was doing his laps before tea.'

Sanderson's face brightened. 'I noticed your swimming pool as we came up the drive. Very impressive. Not like the usual decorative pools some people have in their gardens.'

Professor Collins smiled. 'It's a swimmer's pool,' he said. 'I've been swimming since I was a boy, and the pool is the main reason we stay out here. My eyesight is likely to give out long before my heart or lungs. I'm faltering a bit, but I still do thirty laps a day. My GP says I'm healthier than he is, and he's only fifty-five.'

Baxter finished his cake and stood up. 'Well, I think we must be going,' he said, 'but thank you very much for seeing us, and for these refreshments. We appreciate your assistance.'

Professor Collins helped his wife to her feet and said, 'I know you can't give us any details, but both of us hope you find out what happened to Paula as soon as possible. We gather from the media reports that you suspect foul play, but we just can't imagine that anyone would wish her harm.'

'One of our liaison officers will let you know of any developments,' Baxter said at the doorway, and then he and Sanderson headed for his car. As they neared the main road Baxter told Sanderson to mark Collins as 'unlikely' in his notes and explained why. 'Think we should risk Station Road again, or should we take the A34?' he asked.

'We've got over half an hour to get to North Exton,' Sanderson replied. 'The A34 can get jammed with lorries at this time of day, so Station Road is probably our best bet. Do you really think one of these professors poisoned Mrs Evans, sir?'

'At the moment, they're the most likely source of the warfarin that did kill her, or more specifically, those among them who, unlike Collins, have medical conditions requiring warfarin,' Baxter replied. 'How that warfarin got into her system is another matter.'

* * *

The next two professors they interviewed both ended up as 'likely' in Sanderson's notes, and neither seemed to share the Collins's high opinion of Mrs Evans. Nor did the one wife they met.

Hugo Thompson, Professor of Mathematics and Fellow of Lichfield, apologized for not standing up to greet them when his wife Justine ushered them into the living room of their home in Wittenham Road. 'I'm under doctor's orders to take it easy,' he'd said, 'and since I don't want another heart attack I do his bidding. Please sit down. I suppose you think I can provide you with useful information about Mrs Evans's death, but you're wrong. She was just a secretary who handled some of my correspondence and other paperwork so I could get on with more important things. I hired her about six months ago, when I got out of hospital. She never did get the hang of my filing system and was always fumbling around in one file drawer or another.'

'And she was never on time,' Mrs Thompson added. 'I had

to let her in, of course, and I was late for quite a few engagements. She suggested once that we give her a door key, but that was out of the question. Not even my cleaner has a key, and she's been working for us for decades.'

'According to her diary, she last came here on the afternoon of Friday, July 10th,' Baxter said. 'That was just two days before her death. Did either of you notice anything different about her?'

Mrs Thompson looked startled. 'You know, she actually apologized for being twenty minutes late that day. Said she'd been detained at the Avery-Hills' house. Now that I think about it, she did seem a bit different, sort of bright and chirpy. Usually she was, well, rather reserved, almost grumpy. Don't you agree, Hugo?'

Her husband shrugged his shoulders. 'Can't say I paid much attention to her,' he muttered.

Baxter thanked them for their time, and Mrs Thompson escorted him and Sanderson to the front door. 'Poor Hugo,' she said. 'He's only been able to write three academic papers since his attack, and now he has to spend precious time finding a new secretary.'

'I expect all the medications he has to take are slowing him down, too,' Baxter said in his most sympathetic tone of voice.

'Eleven tablets a day!' Mrs Thompson exclaimed. 'It's the warfarin that worries me most. It's like rat poison, you know. I dole out Hugo's meds every morning, and I am especially careful with that one.'

'As well you should be,' Baxter responded. Then he and Sanderson made their way back to his car. Baxter sighed as he got behind the wheel. 'Not the warmest of people,' he muttered as he headed up the Abingdon Road for their final interview.

Malcolm Littlewood, Professor of Linguistics and Fellow of Manning, opened the front door and came down the steps as they pulled into the gravelled driveway of his house on Clifton Road. 'I'm afraid my wife is feeling unwell this morning, and she's resting now,' he said after introductions were made. 'We can talk in the summer house in the garden, but I hope it won't take long. Both my wife and I are due for check-ups at the cardiac clinic shortly after lunch.'

'Both of you!' Baxter said with feeling. 'That must be tough. Are you managing all right?'

Littlewood smiled ruefully as he led them around the side of the house. 'Fortunately we have an adult son who is currently unemployed and he has graciously moved back in to look after us in our time of need. He makes a stab at cooking healthy meals and running errands, but it is just a bit chaotic at times. Welcome to my sanctuary,' he said, opening the French doors to an impressively large wooden structure with a peaked roof. Overflowing bookshelves lined the back wall and one of the side walls. A long sofa that had seen better days was set against the other side wall. There was a frayed Persian carpet in front of the desk near the back bookshelves, with two sagging leather armchairs lined up at the far end of it, facing the sofa opposite.

'Melissa, my wife, refers to this as "the dumping ground",' Littlewood said as he gestured to Baxter and Sanderson to be seated in the armchairs, 'but I prefer to think of it as an archive of our life in Exton.' He sat down at one end of the sofa. 'We bought this sofa soon after we married, almost forty years ago. Then the chairs a few years later. We got this carpet at an auction in Wantage back in the early 1980s, and it graced our living room until the kids, or maybe it was the dogs as they claimed, had their way with it. I've written just about everything I've ever published at that desk. The next owners of the property can turn this into a proper summer house after we're gone, but I rather like it the way it is now.'

'I can see why,' said Baxter. 'This is certainly a very comfortable work space.' He paused for a moment and then asked, 'Did Mrs Evans come to see you here or in the house?'

Littlewood seemed to stiffen slightly. 'Ah yes, Paula. My apologies for temporarily forgetting the purpose of your visit. A bit of both, actually. She worked for Melissa, too, you see, keeping the accounts for a little investment club she runs. Paula helped me manage the submissions for a journal I edit. Usually she'd come out here first, then go to see Melissa in the kitchen.'

'And you both were happy with the work she did for you?' asked Baxter.

Littlewood looked down briefly, then returned his gaze to Baxter. 'Things change, you know. There's nothing like an intimation of mortality to put a person in a reflective mood, and Melissa and I each got one about two years ago. She was diagnosed with angina one month and I had a pretty serious heart attack two months later. Paula had been a great boon to both of us until then. She simplified our busy, complicated lives, but she became something of a burden once we contemplated doing away with the non-essentials and enjoying the time remaining to us.'

'In what way a burden?' Baxter asked, leaning forward. 'Surely you were not obligated to continue employing her.'

Littlewood smiled ruefully again. 'I hate to admit it,' he

said, 'but she did make us feel obligated. She was an amazingly manipulative woman, able to whinge effectively about her own plight as a working widow some of the time, and at other times to encourage us to "stay active" so we wouldn't lose the will to live. I'd get one message and Melissa would get the other just about every time she came here this past year or so. I'm saddened by her death, of course, but I have to say I'm relieved I'll never see her again.'

Baxter sat back in his chair. 'Just one further question,' he said. 'According to her diary, she last came here on the afternoon of Thursday, July 9th. How did that meeting go?' He noticed that Littlewood took a deep breath before replying.

'Well, it was a bit more dramatic than usual,' Littlewood answered. 'I said something about handing the journal over to a younger colleague, and she sort of went to pieces and started crying, sobbing uncontrollably. I assured her it would take months to arrange things, and it would be business as usual in the meantime. I also said I'd provide her with the names of several colleagues who might well wish to employ her in my stead. That calmed her down somewhat, and I was finally able to get her on her bike and away down the road.'

'So Mrs Evans didn't see your wife on that occasion?' Baxter asked.

'Oh no,' Littlewood replied quickly. 'Melissa had gone to visit some friends in London that day.'

'Right then,' said Baxter, standing up. 'Thank you very much for seeing us. I think we can find our own way back to the car. And best wishes for your check-ups this afternoon.'

'So what did you think of that?' Baxter asked Sanderson as they headed toward the Northern Park & Ride where Sanderson had left his car.

'Some garden shed!' Sanderson replied. 'My Dad would love a sanctuary as big as that. And Professor Littlewood seemed very nice, certainly a lot nicer than Professor Thompson.'

'No doubt about the shed or the personalities,' said Baxter, 'but I have a hunch Thompson was being more honest with us than Littlewood was.'

* * *

Baxter helped himself to tea from the trolley and strode to the whiteboard at the far end of the staff room. He'd spent the last two hours re-reading interview reports, his own and those written up by colleagues, and he now placed these on a nearby table. 'We're here to discuss the Paula Evans case,' he said, bringing an end to desultory conversation among the four other members of his squad. 'Does anyone think we're dealing with an accidental death or a suicide?'

'I'd say suicide was definitely out, sir,' Sergeant Ali Hussein responded. 'On the basis of everything I've learned the deceased was of sound mind and generally cheerful disposition, looking forward to the future. And warfarin is a carefully controlled pharmaceutical, not something that just anyone can get hold of.'

'Surely accidental poisoning is out of the question, too,' said Inspector Susan Andrews. 'One tablet, or even several, wouldn't be lethal, or at least that's what we've been told.'

'Get back to Louise Mason on that, Susan,' Baxter advised. 'See if she and her forensic team can give us some idea of what a lethal dose would be for someone of Mrs Evans's age and build. Meanwhile, let's consider homicide. I think we all agree it's the strongest possibility.' He wrote 'opportunity' on one side of the whiteboard and 'motive' on the other. 'Let's start with the basics. From reading the reports I conclude that eight of Mrs Evans's clients have serious health problems, not necessarily heart disease, of course. I interviewed Professor Rosen yesterday, and he has rheumatoid arthritis. Professor Sarkovsky is wheelchair-bound after a cycling accident, according to Susan's report. The six others do appear to have heart problems of one sort or another. Thompson's wife mentioned that he was on warfarin, and I think we can assume that Avery-Hill is, too. Why else would he have an INR monitoring device? I'm not sure about either of the Littlewoods. For the moment, let's assume that both of them and these other two, Marsden and Black, are also on warfarin.' He wrote the names on the board below 'opportunity'. 'There's no mention of health problems of any sort in the interview reports for her neighbours and close associates, so let's leave them aside until we get to "motive". Susan, you interviewed Marsden and Black. Any ideas about their meds?'

'I'm afraid not,' the Inspector replied. 'I saw them in their college rooms, and the interviews were a bit rushed as they both had meetings to get to. They each mentioned heart trouble and having to slow down a bit when I asked when and why they'd employed Mrs Evans, but that's as far as I was able to get. Come to think of it, though, there was a little box attached to Black's computer, rather like the one you got from Bates's room.'

'How about Bates, sir?' PC Sam Giles asked. 'We found lots of warfarin in his house. Maybe someone got hold of some of it.'

'Okay,' Baxter said. 'We'll keep Marsden and Black in play

for the time being, along with the others, and Sam, you need to interview Bates's neighbours again. Ask if he had many visitors. Was he as casual about the key to his house as he was with his office key? Let's move on to "motive". Does anybody have any hunches about Mrs Evans's neighbours and associates?'

'They were all pretty positive about her and distressed by her death,' Sergeant Hussein replied. He scrolled through his notes on the computer at his desk and said, 'Except maybe for Mrs Anderson, who lives next door. She liked Mrs Evans, but she did complain about the deceased's cat messing up her garden and killing the occasional bird. That's hardly grounds for murder, is it?'

'You'd be surprised, Ali,' said Baxter. 'Arrange to see her again, and see what you can find out about her health and the health of her nearest and dearest. Now how about the clients? On the basis of the reports, I'd say that all but five of them appear to have been entirely satisfied with Mrs Evans. Susan, you note that Avery-Hill was effusive in his praise of her, and I'd say the same about Collins. Those who weren't include only four on our 'opportunity' list: Thompson, the Littlewoods and Black.'

Sanderson was the first to reply. 'Frequently arriving late at Thompson's house and not comprehending his filing system, not sympathizing with the Littlewoods' health problems. It just doesn't add up to grounds for homicide, sir.'

Inspector Andrews nodded in agreement. 'Professor Black did make some negative comments about Mrs Evans,' she said, 'but they were pretty mild. On the order of "lectured me on unnecessary commas in my drafts" or "always tried to get my views on the latest college gossip".

'Right,' Baxter said. 'Let's all put our minds to finding other grounds, if indeed such grounds exist. We have the beginnings of an "opportunity" column, but we are exceedingly lacking in the "motive" column. I'll now ask Silvia to fill us in on coverage of the case in the local media.'

'Yes, sir!' TVP Abingdon's PR Officer Silvia Tanner replied with her usual gusto. 'The briefing by Inspector Andrews last Monday was reported on local TV and radio, as well as in the next day's *Exton Mail*. Every report mentioned that the police were treating the death as unexplained. Since yesterday morning I've been getting enquiries about the basis for our doubts from some local journalists, and one of them actually asked about poison. Naturally I told them all that we'd arrange a further press conference as and when there were any significant new developments. The case is reported on page 2 of the *Exton Times* today, under the headline "Mystery surrounds death of local woman" and the possibility of poisoning is mentioned in paragraph 3. My office has received numerous calls this afternoon, some even from the national media, but we are definitely in no comment mode.'

Baxter smiled faintly. 'Looks like the collegiate rumour mill is working as I'd hoped,' he said. 'That's it for today. We'll meet again same time tomorrow, and let's hope we've made some real progress by then.'

CHAPTER 14

It had been raining when Akiko, Sir Christopher and Tom set off for Arkwright Manor at 2.15 that Thursday afternoon, but the sky cleared as they neared Faringdon and the gently rolling countryside was once again bathed in sunlight.

'Take the next left, then the second right,' said Sir Christopher, consulting the directions TKA4's personal assistant had faxed him that morning. 'The entrance will be on our left, about 200 yards farther on.'

Moments later they were at an imposing metal gate. Tom pushed the button on the intercom and responded to the disembodied voice that asked him to identify himself with a simple 'We're from Thaddeus Hall'. The gate slowly swung open, and he drove on.

It was another 100 yards down a tree-lined lane before they caught their first glimpse of the house. 'Wow,' said Tom. 'It's beautiful, and huge!'

'Late Georgian, I'd say,' said Sir Christopher, 'and beautiful indeed. Just look at that golden stone, that graceful portico. We Brits did know how to build houses back in the eighteenth century.'

'Rich Brits,' said Tom. 'Don't forget the tiny hovels of the poor.'

Sir Christopher looked at him a bit sharply. 'I am intending to forget that today, son, and I hope you will, too. We're here to further ingratiate ourselves with our sole benefactor, who is a very rich Brit indeed.'

They passed an extensive stable yard and pulled to a stop in the gravelled courtyard in front of the house. A woman in a smart trouser suit opened the front door as they approached.

'Hello,' she said. 'I'm Jenny Palmer, Mr Arkwright's P.A. here in the UK. Do call me Jenny. He's on the phone with New York just now, but his sister, Mrs Adams, is waiting for you in the long gallery upstairs. This way, please.' She led them across the marble-floored entry hall to an imposing staircase, lined with paintings.

'Look at these!' Tom said to Akiko as they climbed the stairs. 'The colours, the depth, the light. I've never seen anything like them.'

'They're by various Canadian artists,' Jenny said. 'Members of the Group of Seven back in the 1920s. They were trying to find a less European way of painting the landscapes around them, I'm told. Mr Arkwright's grandfather bought these eight paintings at an exposition in Toronto when he was on his way to England.' She led them along a wide corridor at the top of the stairs and paused outside an imposing door. 'If you like paintings, you're really going to like what comes next.' She knocked and opened the door.

A trim woman, probably in her mid-sixties, rose to greet them. She was casually dressed in white trousers and a pale blue tunic. Her dark gray hair fell in a soft bob about her face. Behind her, on the walls between narrow windows opening to the north, were two immense paintings of Venice.

'Welcome,' she said warmly. 'I'm Elizabeth Adams, TK's middle sister. Do call me Elizabeth. It is a pleasure to meet you, Ms Sugiyama, and to see you again, Sir Christopher. We did meet briefly at my father's funeral, I recollect. Perhaps this young man you've brought with you would like to take a closer look at our Canalettos?'

'My son Tom,' said Sir Christopher. 'He paints, but he isn't usually so unsociable.'

Hearing his name, Tom was startled back to civility. 'I do apologize,' he said, 'but those are so magnificent. I spent hours in the Uffizi a few years ago trying to figure out how he made the water become so alive.'

'They're from my mother's family,' said Elizabeth. 'Like all the paintings in this room, they're the product of several Grand Tours of the Continent by her forebears. These two are probably from Canaletto's later years, when he was slipping a bit. You'll be able to study them at leisure in the National Gallery soon, Tom. My father's wishes, along with a deal with HMRC to reduce inheritance tax, of course. When this house is sold, which may be very soon, off they go, along with most of the other Grand Tour purchases here. There's nothing else particularly distinguished, although I am very fond of the Onofri over by the door behind you. Such confident brushwork.'

'Do you paint, Elizabeth?' Akiko asked.

'I dabble,' she replied with a smile. 'Mostly watercolours and acrylics.'

'And will you be visiting here for long?' asked Sir Christopher as they all sat down.

'Actually I've been living here for the past six years or so,' Elizabeth replied. 'Ever since my husband died. I looked after my father in his last years, and then I stayed on to look after the house as best I could. But this place needs to be filled with people, gaiety, life. That will be the case next month when my children and grandchildren visit for a few weeks, but then it will become a museum again. A very orderly museum at that: eighteenth century and somewhat earlier in this room, Canadians on the stairway, impressionists in the dining room. My father loved art, but he went about enjoying it in much too organized a manner for my taste. No, when the sale goes through, I'll move back to my flat in London.'

'Yes, of course,' said Sir Christopher. 'This is an exquisite house in a lovely part of Extonshire, but rather isolated. It must be hard to get to the theatre, to see friends. Even Exton can be rather limiting at times. That's why I'm planning to go back to my place in Notting Hill when I retire in a couple of years' time.'

'Notting Hill!' exclaimed Elizabeth. 'I'm just minutes away in Holland Park. We'll be neighbours.'

Just then TKA4 strode into the room. 'My dear Akiko, my dear Warden!' he said in a loud voice. 'I am so sorry to have kept you waiting. Shall we head downstairs to the library? Jenny has the acquisition records we talked about last night all laid out for us.'

Elizabeth looked over at Tom. 'Care for a little tour?' she asked.

'Oh yes!' Tom replied. 'The dining room certainly sounds interesting.'

'It is indeed,' she said. 'Come, let's be off.' She took his hand and led him to the door to the back stairway at the far end of the room.

* * *

Several ledgers rested on the large oak desk in the library.

Akiko opened the one labelled *Japan 1* to its first page. '1948,' she said. 'Midway through the post-war Occupation. Those were desperate times in Japan, and a lot of people, including aristocrats and members of zaibatsu families, were selling off their treasures just to survive. This three-panelled screen sounds intriguing. If it really is seventeenth century, it's worth a lot more than the $250 your father paid for it. This Raku tea bowl, too. And this Old Arita plate. Do these numbers in the margins refer to photos?'

'Yes,' said Jenny. 'An entire digital inventory was made three years ago for insurance purposes.'

'Well, if you send me photocopies of, say, these first twenty pages, up to his third trip in 1959, and the photos for the items listed, I can show them to a friend at our national museum. Strictly in confidence, of course. I won't mention the Arkwright name. My friend worked closely in the late 1980s with a group of Japanese who were trying to track down important cultural properties that had left the country after the war and bring them home. They advertised via veterans' organizations in the States mostly and purchased quite a number of things. Fine ceremonial swords, as you might expect, but also some wonderful hanging scrolls, chests and tea bowls. And they paid their owners good prices, much higher than they could have got locally. If my friend finds anything interesting, he'll let me know, and I'll get back to you. You'd probably make a lot more selling through him than at auction in London.' She smiled at TKA4. 'I don't suppose I could have a look at item 17?' she asked. 'It's listed as Old Kutani, and I come from a family of Kutani porcelain painters in Nomi.'

'You may indeed, my dear Akiko,' said TKA4. He opened

one of the drawers of the desk and pressed a button inside it. A bookcase at the end of the room slowly opened, revealing a dimly lit room beyond. 'This way to my father's inner sanctum,' he said, taking her arm.

'Oh my,' Akiko whispered as she stepped inside. The room was at least fifteen feet wide and twenty-five feet deep. The wall on one side was lined with archive drawers; the wall on the other side, with display cases. An exquisite wooden Bodhisattva smiled enigmatically from the far end. She paused at a drawer labelled 'netsuke'. 'May I?' she asked.

'By all means,' said TKA4. 'There are dozens of them in there. Frankly, I can't see what's so appealing about them.'

Akiko slid the drawer open and gazed admiringly at the intricate carving on the tiny objects before her. 'Oh look,' she said. 'What charming little monkeys, having such a good time scrambling all over one another. It must have taken months to carve this.' She lifted the *netsuke* to her cheek. 'Very cool, definitely ivory,' she said. 'They're almost more popular in the West now than in Japan. I suggest you contact Jeremy Coates in London. He's on the list I prepared for you this morning. Here it is.' Akiko reached into her handbag and gave TKA4 a sheet of paper. 'I expect he'll tell you that you can get more for them individually than as a collection. I took the liberty of including the name of one of my Interpol contacts in Paris, just down here. We've had some complaints about agencies that supply contemporary art works in bulk, so you may wish to have Jenny check with him about the agency you're dealing with for your Dubai villa. My own contact details are on the attached card.'

Next to catch Akiko's eye was a drawer marked 'Russo-Japanese War triptychs'. She slid the drawer open and removed the covering paper from the first of perhaps six prints in the drawer, three scenes depicting the victory of the Japanese fleet over the Russian fleet at Tsushima in 1905. 'If the others are in the same fine condition as this one,' she said, 'several museums in Japan will be interested in them. Not to mention collectors in this part of the world. Putting them up at auction is probably your best bet. The same with all the other woodblock prints filed here,' she said as she glanced at the labels on other drawers. One famous artist after another: Hiroshige, Hokusai, Kunisada, Utamaro…

'Stefan Wold – he's also on my list – can advise you on those and put you in touch with the right people at the V&A and British Museum,' Akiko said. 'I'm sure you are well aware of the tax advantages of charitable donations, especially in a year when you sell a major property in the UK.'

She turned to the display cases as Jenny opened the third of them and extracted item 17. 'Oh,' sighed Akiko as she examined the shallow round plate that Jenny now handed her, 'one of my favourite "bird and flower" designs! Such a cheeky kingfisher here on the bamboo branch and such lovely chrysanthemums and wild grasses lower down.' She paused for a moment before continuing. 'Hmm. There's definitely a pale blueish tinge to the unpainted porcelain. The enamels on the design are a bit worn, but I think there's just a hint of red down here among the grasses. Perhaps some wildflowers?' She reversed the plate and found no mark. Turning to TKA4 she said, 'You may have a real treasure here, Mr Arkwright. This just might be a real Old Kutani dish dating from the late 17th century, not a Yoshidaya 19th-century revival of the same basic design. If so, it's incredibly valuable. You see, no red enamel was ever used on Yoshidaya porcelain and most of the pieces made at that kiln had a "Good Fortune" mark on the underside. This one just has a few slash marks. But that said, even if it is Yoshidaya, it is still very rare – and in such good condition, too! May I mention it to a colleague in Japan? He would jump at the chance to come and take a look at it, I'm sure.'

'Of course,' said TKA4. 'To me, it's just another one of these pretty little things my father collected. Have your colleague get in touch with Jenny, and she will arrange a viewing. Then we can discuss terms. That three-panelled screen you mentioned earlier is in my dressing room upstairs. Very useful for airing shirts. Shall we go have a look at it?'

* * *

After tea in the garden room, everyone gathered in the courtyard for farewells. It was almost 6.00, and long shadows were cast on the gravel.

'Thanks for all those tips, Akiko,' TKA4 said effusively. 'I have a hunch you will be both making and saving me money. And I'll be in touch with you as soon as the house is sold, Chris, about that bursary fund we discussed yesterday. Maybe we can squeeze a bit in for your doctoral students after all.'

'And I'll be seeing you on Saturday afternoon, Tom,' said Elizabeth. 'About 3.00?' She turned to Sir Christopher. 'I'm having lunch with an old school friend in Exton, and your son has kindly agreed to show me some of his work. His comments on mine have been most helpful.'

'I see,' said Sir Christopher. 'I'm sure you'll have some useful comments for him, too, and I do hope you will stay on for tea with us at the Lodgings.'

'I'd be delighted,' said Elizabeth.

Akiko could scarcely contain herself as they drove down the lane, and she was laughing long before they reached the gate.

'Whatever is this all about?' asked Sir Christopher, looking back at her from the front seat.

'It's about you two,' she said once she had managed to regain a degree of composure. 'Father and son being charmed by and charming the same woman. What a double act you are!'

Tom winked at Akiko in the rear-view mirror, but Sir Christopher remained puzzled. 'We merely exchanged the usual pleasantries,' he said.

'Loosen up, Dad,' Tom said as he turned onto the main road back to Exton. 'You know you were being particularly nice to her. She's very good-looking, and soon to be your neighbour in London now that you've strangely decided against a quiet life in the countryside. And what paintings they have back there! An early Monet and some good Pissarros in the dining room, two Constables in the drawing room, a Matisse in one of the guest bedrooms! Not to mention those late but still wonderful Canalettos. I'm keen to have another look at the Canadian landscapes, too. And on top of all that, her watercolours are very good. I'm hoping to learn a thing or two from her on Saturday.'

'Hmm,' said Sir Christopher. 'I see. Well, far be it from me to interfere with your education in art and art history. And Elizabeth certainly is much more pleasant to be with than her brother. Perhaps I should invite her to High Table at TH sometime in the fall, before she decamps to London.'

'Her brother is horrible!' said Akiko with feeling. 'How

could he be so dismissive of all those beautiful Japanese pieces he has? And what about his father, supposed lover of Japanese art, locking everything away in that sterile prison? It was hard for me to remain civil and accommodating, I can assure you, Chris. Still, it will have been worth it if some of those pieces, especially that lovely Kutani plate, get freed into more caring and sharing hands.'

'With apologies for being so crassly materialistic, what do you suppose that Japanese collection back there is worth?' Sir Christopher asked.

'The Raku bowl and Old Kutani plate are easily worth about £100,000 each,' Akiko replied. 'That three-panelled screen could be worth a bit more, despite the damage to it from his coat hangers. The Bodhisattva could well be even more valuable. And then there's all the "delicate and pale stuff" like the *netsuke*. Not to mention the woodblock prints. Pretty close to £700,000, I'd say at a guess.'

'I see,' said Sir Christopher. 'I think I'd better put the Bursar into the frame about this, get him involved in monitoring the sales and reminding TKA4 of his promise to us. We probably need to get something in writing straight away.'

CHAPTER 15

Early Friday morning. Akiko sat at the table in Baxter's kitchen, her chin resting on her folded hands. She was wearing one of his t-shirts, which hung loosely about her shoulders and covered her to well below her hips. 'I could get used to being waited on,' she said as Baxter, clad only in jeans, placed a toasted muffin and a mug of coffee in front of her.

'Breakfast is a snap,' he replied as he sat down next to her, 'but it's my limit so far as cooking is concerned. Where shall we go for dinner tonight?'

'Why don't I make us dinner,' Akiko said. 'Maybe some fish? I could go into town...' Her voice broke and she covered her face with her hands. 'We have so little time left,' she murmured.

Baxter pulled her onto his lap and cradled her in his arms. 'Akiko my sweet, please don't go wobbly on me,' he said softly. 'If it wasn't for this homicide, we never would have found each other, you know. We'll work something out. You'd have to go a lot farther away than Tokyo to be shut of me.'

Akiko leaned against his shoulder and breathed deeply. 'What does "go wobbly" mean?' she asked.

'Ah,' said Baxter, 'a chink at last in your command of my native language. To "go wobbly" is to falter,' he continued as he stroked her hair, 'to lose hope, to give up.'

'Oh, I see,' said Akiko as she took one last deep breath,

raised her head and looked into his eyes. Such concerned, deep blue-green eyes. 'Well, I wasn't "going wobbly". Maybe I was heading in the direction of a wobble, but I'm sure I would have stopped in time. And I have no intention of going an inch farther away from you than Tokyo.'

'That's my girl,' said Baxter, kissing her on her nose. He had just slipped his hand under her t-shirt onto her thigh when the fax machine on the kitchen counter whirred into operation. Akiko sighed and stood up. 'Go on,' she said. 'I'm just as curious as you are to know what it says.'

Baxter retrieved the fax and brought it back to the table. 'Hmm, looks like we might have some connections. See here? Two of the wives are from County Durham, same as Bates, and one of them is Mrs Avery-Hill! Née Davis. Her father was a solicitor in Darlington, and that's where Bates's father had his dental practice. The fathers could well have known each other, and maybe their kids were acquainted, too.'

The fax whirred again. 'Bless you, Stella,' Baxter said as he read the text. 'She's searched *The Northern Echo* on the newspaper database. Daphne Elisabeth Davis went off to read history at Atkins College here in Exton in 1968. Bates was a graduate student at Dunstan then. The "swinging sixties". Do you suppose he fell for her? Loved her and lost? I have a hunch this is going to be a very good day, and Professor Winston Avery-Hill is just going to have to put up with seeing me again if he's at home when I drop by.'

He swept Akiko into his arms and twirled her around the kitchen. 'But I'm not off to work just yet,' he said as he came to a sudden stop and released her. 'Where were we before that first fax arrived?'

'I think you were trying to get your t-shirt back,' Akiko replied demurely.

'So I was!' Baxter said. 'You are so very observant, Akiko. Do you mind if that's one of the reasons why I like you so very much?'

'No, not in the least,' Akiko said as she leaned against his chest. 'After all, your great enthusiasm for solving crime is one of the reasons why I like you so very much.'

Baxter put his arms around her and held her tightly for a moment. Then he lifted her up and carried her off to his bed.

* * *

It was almost 11.00 am when Baxter pulled into the driveway at the Lodgings. He gave Akiko a lingering kiss.

'You're late for work,' she said.

'It may have escaped your attention,' he replied, 'but we did do a little work on the case back at my place earlier this morning.'

'Oh, yes, so we did,' she said, as she opened the car door. 'Well, I'll head into town soon and get us some nice fish for dinner. Maybe some strawberries, too.'

'And I'm off to *chercher la femme*,' Baxter said with a sigh.

Akiko frowned slightly. '*La femme*,' she said quietly, staring at the windscreen.

'Sorry,' Baxter said. 'I only did 0-level French.'

Akiko looked at him. 'Oh no, it's not your pronunciation. *La*, that's the singular. It could be *les femmes*, you know.'

Baxter stared at her. 'Crikey, you may be right!' he said after a moment's thought. 'That would certainly explain a few things that have been troubling us about Mrs Evans's death.'

He reached over and stroked her face. 'So beautiful, so clever,' he murmured. 'And you like me. I can't believe my luck.' He kissed her again.

'Until tonight then,' Akiko said softly as she got out of the car.

Tom and a rather attractive young woman had just reached the bottom of the stairs when Akiko unlocked the front door and stepped into the entry hall. Tom was clad only in jeans, and the young woman apparently wore nothing other than a light blue Cambridge t-shirt.

Tom, just slightly flustered, made the introductions. 'Hi, Akiko,' he said, 'This is my friend Michelle, Michelle Barton. Michelle, this is Akiko Sugiyama, who is visiting us from Tokyo.'

Akiko smiled benignly at them both. 'Such a wonderful day, isn't it?' she said as she made her way upstairs to her room.

'My mother is like that sometimes,' said Michelle as she and Tom headed for the kitchen. 'It's a sure sign she and Dad have just had good sex. Not often enough, though. I've tried, but she just won't talk about it with me. I don't suppose you and your father talk much about sex?'

'Not since I was about eleven,' said Tom as he handed her a mug of tea. 'But I'm pretty sure he's getting his fair share.'

'Actually,' said Michelle, 'there's some very interesting anthropological literature on transgenerational sex talk. It seems that the more complex the culture, the less such talk there is between parents and children.'

'Okay,' said Tom, 'but who's doing the talking? If it's just the parents telling the children what's right, then females are likely to end up with a raw deal, aren't they? Here, at least, girls have a chance to explore a bit on their own.'

'That's a good point, Tom,' Michelle said, 'but look what time it is! I'd better get going.' She smiled at him. 'It was good this morning,' she said. 'Your sensitivity to the needs of girls is much appreciated. Text me whenever, otherwise I'll see you next Friday morning.' She gave him a kiss, tousled his hair and headed upstairs to his room to retrieve her clothes.

CHAPTER 16

Midday on Friday. Baxter parked on the street outside the Avery-Hills' large house on Berrick Road in North Exton, walked up the driveway and rang the doorbell. After a minute or so the door was opened by a tall, slender woman with striking grey eyes and short chestnut brown hair. Almost sixty, Baxter figured, and very well-preserved.

'Yes?' Daphne Avery-Hill asked.

Baxter identified himself, showed his ID and asked if he might speak to her briefly.

'Surely it is my husband you wish to see,' she replied briskly, 'but he is not here at the moment. Lucky for him, I might add, if you're the same DCI who interrogated him last week.'

'I confess that I am,' Baxter said, relieved that the professor was away, 'and I was very pleased to learn from a colleague yesterday that he is now back in fine form. But actually it is you I'd like to talk to. I'm trying to tie up some loose ends concerning the death of Theodore Bates, and I thought you might be able to help.'

'I see,' Daphne said. 'Poor Theo. I expect you already know something of our past or you wouldn't be here. Do come in. I've just finished doing a bit of gardening and was making myself some coffee. Let's talk in the kitchen.' She led him to a spacious room at the back of the house and gestured to a chair at the kitchen table. 'Milk or sugar?' she asked as she placed two mugs on the counter.

'Milk, no sugar,' Baxter replied as he sat down. 'Quite a view of your garden from here, and quite a garden.'

Daphne handed him a mug and sat down opposite. 'We get lots of visitors on our Open Day during Exton's Garden Week every June, certainly more than anyone else in the neighbourhood. So, what would you like to know about me and Theo?'

Baxter swiftly decided that it was best to match her direct approach with his own. 'Did you know him back in Darlington before you came up to Exton?' he asked.

Daphne smiled at him. 'My, you have been doing your homework, haven't you? Our parents were friends, so I expect we met as children from time to time. But he was five years older than I was and not the least bit interested in little girls. He and my older brother went to the same school and got along quite well.'

'And once you became a student here?' Baxter asked.

'He was finishing up his doctorate then, and he gave a small group of us at Atkins some revision classes in English history for our Mods exams,' Daphne replied. 'I seduced him. It made studying the Tudors so much more interesting.'

'I see,' said Baxter, noting that she was enjoying their conversation. 'And then?'

Daphne smiled at him again. 'And then he insisted we get engaged. Theo was so impossibly serious about everything, so out of step with the times. Most of us were just having fun in bed. It was the late 60s, after all. I expect you were still a boy back then, Inspector, but for those of us a bit older it was fantastic. Especially for us girls. Away from home for the first time or from the ghastly private schools our parents had sent us to, vastly outnumbered by the male students here at Exton. And, of course, those of us in the know could get the pill. There were some girls at Atkins who were intent on getting good degrees and having careers, but I was not one of them.'

'So why the engagement?' Baxter asked, hoping his hunch that it had occurred was correct.

Daphne laughed again. 'Well, I wanted a degree of some sort, however marginal, and I was told at the start of my third year that I was in danger of failing Finals. Daddy had promised me a car as a graduation present, so I needed Theo's help once more. And so we got engaged. He'd just become Lecturer in Medieval History at TH. Over the next few months he gave me a crash course in everything I had only studied in the most superficial manner and I ended up with an almost respectable lower second. He was not the best of lovers, but he was a fine teacher.'

'You needn't go into the details unless you want to,' Baxter said, 'but surely it must have been difficult for Theo to have found himself a colleague of the man you did end up marrying.'

Daphne looked down at her coffee mug briefly and then returned her gaze to Baxter. 'Theo should have got over it long ago. It's not my fault that he didn't. Winston swept into Exton in the summer of 1971, just after Finals, having got himself the first-ever Arkwright Post-doctoral Fellowship at TH, and he swept me off my feet at one of the college balls I went to. Are you married, Inspector?'

'I used to be,' Baxter replied.

'Well, Winston and I have now been married for almost forty years, and that's because I got the chemistry right. I would have been bored with Theo within a year or two, so in breaking off our engagement I was doing him a favour. And I did try over the years to introduce him to suitable women. I have the impression he fell for at least one of them, but nothing came of it.'

'So you continued to see him socially?' Baxter asked.

'Of course,' Daphne said. 'Not just at college events and the occasional dinner party, but at garden club meetings, too. He was an excellent plantsman, and I got lots of lovely cuttings from him.'

'How did you know he hadn't got over you?' Baxter asked.

Daphne gave him a vaguely pitying look. 'Really, Inspector. Because it was blindingly obvious, that's why. I didn't encourage him in any way, of course.'

'No, of course not,' Baxter said. 'I wasn't suggesting anything of the sort. Well, many thanks for your time and the coffee. Just one further question so long as I'm here. You'll be aware that we are also investigating the death of Paula Evans. Did you see much of her in the years she was working for your husband?'

Baxter caught just the slightest hint of a stiffening of her shoulders, a narrowing of her eyes, but Daphne was soon her confident self again. 'Winston needed a secretary,' she said, 'but why he chose Mrs Evans has always baffled me. She was quite common, if you know what I mean. Terrible taste in clothes, too much make-up. I had as little to do with her as possible.'

Baxter took his leave and drove back to Abingdon. He spent the early afternoon filling out evaluation forms on his subordinates and was relieved to get to the case meeting at 4.00. 'Okay, everyone,' he said as he made his way to the whiteboard in the staff room. 'Let's hear your progress reports in the Paula Evans case.'

'I think we can rule out Mrs Anderson,' Sergeant Hussein said. 'She's in good health, as are her kith and kin, and she's even thinking of adopting the deceased's "poor little kitty". Apparently it came begging for attention at her back door a few days ago and she realized there was now no one to feed it. The cat was sleeping on one of the chairs in her living room while we spoke, so I'd say the adoption is a done deal.'

PC Giles then reported on Bates. 'He had students round for drinks maybe three times a term, according to one of his neighbours, but that was about the extent of his entertaining. After a burglary some six years ago he had a proper mortice lock fitted on his front door and a combination lock put on his side gate, according to another neighbour. He'd told that neighbour he had a key to the back door buried somewhere in the garden, but the neighbour didn't know precisely where. He didn't have a regular cleaner. Instead he'd get one of those cleaning firms in two or three times a year to do a blitz clean, and he was always on hand to make sure they didn't touch any of the papers on his desk. It was there, in a desk drawer, that we found his unused warfarin tablets.'

Inspector Andrews read from her computer screen. 'Louise apologizes that she can't be more precise, but she estimates that Mrs Evans had about 15 mg of warfarin in her system at post-mortem. That's equivalent to three times the full dose an adult would take daily. Not nearly enough to do the damage found to her internal organs, however. That might have required twenty or more full-dose tablets over a relatively short period of time, say a few weeks. They'd found opened packages of aspirin and ibuprofen in her medicine cabinet.

Both could have intensified the effects of the warfarin, but they don't know how frequently she took either of them. For what it's worth, Louise could find no documented cases of deliberate warfarin poisoning on the Net, although it has been suggested that's how Beria and maybe some other Politburo members did Josef Stalin in back in the 1950s.'

Baxter turned to the whiteboard. 'Okay,' he said. 'We'll put a question mark after Bates in the opportunity column and strike Mrs Anderson from the motive column. Let's add the Avery-Hills to the latter. The professor himself was full of praise for Mrs Evans when Susan saw him on Wednesday, but I saw his wife earlier today and she had some negative things to say about her. No more incriminating than any of the other negative comments we've heard to date, but like Littlewood her body language suggested a bit more animosity than she revealed.'

'So what do you suggest?' Susan Andrews asked. 'Shall we up the pressure on our might-have-motive list and hope for a break?'

'That's our only option at the moment,' Baxter conceded. 'I'm on duty tomorrow. Who else?' Sergeant Hussein, DC Sanderson and PC Giles raised their hands. 'Right then. Ali, get on the phone now and arrange follow-up interviews as early in the day as possible with the Thompsons and Avery-Hills. Take Sam with you,' Baxter said. 'Sandy, you get us appointments with the Marsdens, the Blacks and the Littlewoods. Tell all of them that there has been a new development in the Evans case, and we'd appreciate their help with our enquiries. If any of them mention the piece in the *Exton Times* just say that we're prepared to discuss that when we meet.'

'Give me a call if you need me,' Susan Andrews said as she and Baxter left the staff room. 'It's not very promising, is it?'

'Not at the moment,' Baxter acknowledged. 'But one never knows. And thanks for the offer of help. In the admittedly unlikely event that we get a break I may well ask you to handle the media. You're so much more telegenic than I am.'

'Thank you, James,' she replied. 'I am going to quote that to my husband as soon as I get home.'

CHAPTER 17

Friday evening about 8.00. Baxter sat at his kitchen table sipping a glass of Chablis and watching admiringly as Akiko, at the sink, shelled and deveined the ten langoustines she had just parboiled. The Japanese rice she had tracked down at an oriental grocery store was steaming in a covered pot on the hob. Three foil-wrapped salmon filets basted with lemon juice, minced ginger and a dash of soy sauce were roasting in the oven.

She smiled at him. 'I'll just do the salad and stir-fry the langoustines with these green onions for a moment or two, and then we'll eat. We're having fusion tonight: great British ingredients cooked somewhat in the Asian way, plus lovely English strawberries for dessert. I'll do Japanese food for you in Tokyo. It's so much easier there. Your fishmonger in the Old Market is good, but mine is better, and I have better knives and a lot more pots and pans than you have.'

Baxter caught her by the waist as she passed by and pulled her toward him. 'You're spoiling me, and I love it,' he said.

'Of course I am,' she replied as she kissed him on his forehead and continued toward the refrigerator. 'You can spoil me back at breakfast. Besides, I really do like to cook. It's a way of unwinding, you know, and so much more immediately rewarding than some of the other things I do all day. And there's so much space here in your kitchen! Mine is tiny. We'd be bumping into each other at every turn if both of us were in there at the same time.'

'Now that's an interesting prospect,' said Baxter. 'I do like bumping into you. You smell so temptingly fresh, like a ripe apple on the tree.'

Akiko laughed as she arranged the food on their plates. 'We had a teacher in high school who warned us girls about men like you,' she said. 'I'd almost given up hope of ever meeting one.' She put the plates on the table and sat down opposite him.

Baxter refilled their wine glasses. 'So I'm the lecherous male of your dreams?' he asked as he raised a langoustine to his mouth.

'To that teacher you would have been a lecher, a threat to females throughout Ishikawa prefecture, which was the extent of her world. But, no, that's not what I meant. It's that you're so relaxed about sex, and so good at it,' Akiko replied, smiling at him. 'I find it quite liberating.' She chewed a piece of salmon thoughtfully. 'My husband and I had some good times together long ago, but we were so very young, such innocents. We were still fumbling with the basics when he was killed.'

'And Peter?' Baxter asked gently.

Akiko took a sip of Chablis. 'Peter was good in bed, no doubt about that. But that was pretty much the extent of our intimacy. We went out a lot, to gallery openings, parties at one embassy or another, but only very rarely just the two of us for a quiet dinner somewhere. We talked about art or art crime, not about ourselves. It didn't seem so strange to me at the time. Maybe I was too involved in my work to notice. Or maybe I got more involved in my work so I wouldn't notice.' She looked across the table at Baxter. 'It's so different with you, James. Yes, we've talked about this case a bit, but so much more than that. You keep in touch with me with words, gestures, those wonderful eyes of yours. I've never felt so comfortable, so free in being with someone. More salad?'

Baxter took the bowl she held out and helped himself. 'This dinner is terrific,' he said as he speared a final chunk of salmon with his fork. 'Why is this rice so much better than the rice I get at my favourite Chinese restaurant?'

'This rice is better because it's Japanese rice, or rather California rice of the Japanese sort. And you saw how easy it was to do the salmon,' Akiko replied. 'You could make it yourself. Much better for you than all those microwave meals you keep in the freezer.'

'Now you're trying to make a modern male of me,' said Baxter. 'That's going to be a tough one, I'm afraid. Couldn't you be content with a man who likes absolutely everything about you, including your cooking?' He sat back and gazed at her. 'Don't give me all the credit, Akiko. We were ready for each other. And our minds do work in similar ways. That's why it's so good between us. We've both had enough experience and enough honesty to confront the things that went wrong for us that, well, the rest was pretty easy. After you helped me invite you out to dinner the other day, that is.'

'You did need just a bit of help,' Akiko said as she refilled their glasses.

'That's true,' said Baxter, munching a bite of salad. 'The rules seem to have changed during the nineteen years I was married. I was pretty good at chatting girls up when I was in my early twenties. Try that now, and I'd likely be done for sexual harassment. No, almost all the women I've had casual affairs with since the divorce made the first move on me, and I just responded appropriately.'

'You felt safer keeping things casual, I expect,' Akiko said.

Baxter sighed. 'I did indeed. Losing Helen really hit me hard. You know, when I first moved into this flat I used to sit at this very table for hours at night, drinking too much whisky and trying to figure out why our marriage had failed. I didn't like being alone, but I didn't want to risk the pain of losing someone again either.' He toyed with the remaining salad leaves on his plate. 'I saw Helen briefly from time to time when I collected our son for a day out, but we spent quite a bit of time together at our daughter's wedding five years ago. Her husband was with her. The man she left me for because "he really loves me". They'd been married for maybe six years then, and I could see he loved her by the way he looked at her, I could hear it in his tone of voice when he spoke to her. They were connected in the way that she and I had once been connected, way back when we first got together, but I'd let that slip away while I concentrated on rising up through the ranks at TVP. God, I envied him. Not for having her, but for having a life. I realized then that I wanted a life, too. I wanted to be my whole self again, not just a good detective and agreeable date. I probably started looking at women a bit differently after that, looking for someone I could get really close to, but nothing clicked until I met you.'

'I'll get the strawberries,' Akiko said.

Baxter stood up. 'No, I'll get them. You tell me more about this tiny place of yours in Tokyo.'

'Only the kitchen is tiny!' Akiko protested. 'It's a lovely, quiet apartment in Naka-Meguro, with a wonderful view of a nearby park from the balcony, and all just forty minutes from my office. It's practically the same size as your flat here. It's tough for families in Tokyo, but you should see some of the cramped "rabbit hutches" my married friends have in Manhattan. I bought my place back in the mid-1990s after the bubble burst and property prices went down a good notch or two. And I redecorated it last summer after Peter left. He liked bright colours and insisted on western furniture. Now it's a lot less cluttered and softer in tone. There are tatami mats back in the main room. I have a few fine pieces of Kutani from my father's collection and a wonderful old chest that was part of my mother's dowry. Umm, these strawberries are delicious, aren't they?'

'You commute forty minutes each way?' Baxter asked. 'How can you stand it? I can barely put up with a ten-minute drive to work.'

'What a sheltered existence you people lead here in Extonshire,' said Akiko. 'There are more than twelve million of us in Tokyo, and not everyone can live just a few minutes from work. Fortunately, I usually have the freedom to travel before or after rush hour. A brief walk at each end of the trip and a 27-minute ride on the subway in between. Sometimes I read on the subway, but mostly I study the people around me. I confess that I eavesdrop on their conversations and imagine their lives.'

'Ah,' said Baxter. 'Honing your detection skills, which are quite impressive, I must say. And these mats? This absence of furniture?'

'Just you wait and see,' said Akiko. 'Tatami mats are soft, they give just a bit beneath the bare foot, smell slightly sweet. It is the most sensuous flooring imaginable. Sometimes on a hot summer night I open the doors to my balcony, turn off all the lights and lie down on one of the mats naked, breathing its fragrance in and thinking about all those apples just beginning to ripen out in the countryside. There are floor cushions covered in beautifully patterned silk and soft futon to sleep on. And one easy chair left in the dining room, where I sometimes sit reading until late at night. You may sit there while I get our bath ready in my deep tub. There's just enough room for two.'

'A very stimulating answer to my questions,' said Baxter, grinning at her. 'The bit about ripening apples was particularly moving. But Naka-Meguro is far away, and my bedroom is just over there. How about we try to make the best of it right now on good old British cotton sheets?'

The phone rang just as they had both stood up and clasped hands. 'Damn!' said Baxter. He snatched the phone from its stand. 'Yes?' he said. 'I see. I remember the address. Twenty minutes? Right, see you at 9.30. Wait for me on the road.' He put the phone back and turned to Akiko. 'That was Sanderson. We seem to have got a break in the case. Professor Littlewood has just phoned in and said his wife has something to tell us. I've got to go.'

'Of course you do,' said Akiko. 'I'll be here when you get back.'

'Stay off those strawberries while I'm gone,' he said, enfolding her in a passionate embrace. 'They're dynamite.'

* * *

Melissa Littlewood took her husband's hand in hers when he sat down beside her on the sofa in their well-appointed living room. Baxter and Sanderson sat down opposite in easy chairs.

'You asked to see us,' Baxter said in an even tone of voice.

Melissa looked straight at him. 'I didn't mean to kill her,' she said. 'I just wanted to make her go away, to leave us alone. I'm so sorry.'

Baxter could see that she was struggling to retain her composure. 'Perhaps you could be a bit more explicit,' he said gently. 'What exactly did you do to make her go away?'

Melissa tightened her grip on her husband's hand and took a deep breath. 'I put one of Malcolm's warfarin tablets in her tea every time she came here. They'd made Malcolm so queasy when he first started taking them, so I thought they'd have the same effect on her. Make her a bit ill, you know, so she'd stay at home. But she kept coming.'

'And when did you start doing this?' Baxter asked.

'About three months ago, I think,' Melissa replied, wiping away a tear with her free hand. 'Just after...'

'Just after I'd told Melissa about the blackmail,' the professor interjected, 'and the reason for it.'

Baxter felt his pulse quicken, but his voice was steady when he spoke. 'Mrs Evans was blackmailing you?' he asked.

Littlewood nodded. 'For about three years,' he said, eyes downcast. 'I'd had an affair, a very brief affair, with one of my graduate students, and she'd found out about it somehow. Probably by reading my email when I went up to the house to get something or go to the loo. She said she'd keep quiet if I doubled what I was paying her. At the time it seemed a good way of preserving my marriage and my reputation. Then last March she asked for a £3,000 "contribution" toward her planned trip around the world. I told her that was impossible. I could absorb the extra salary to her from the editorial fees I received from the journal, but a one-off payment on that scale would have to come from my personal accounts, all of which are joint with Melissa. That's when I decided to come clean with Melissa and stop the whole thing.'

'But nothing would stop her,' Melissa said with some bitterness. 'Even after I informed her that Malcolm had told me everything and that all was well between us, she kept at it. "You two may have sorted things out," she said, "but what about his college and the University? Think of the damage to his career if this became known. He could even be forced to resign." That's when I started putting the tablets in her tea every time I saw her.'

Littlewood looked at Baxter. 'Is there some way Melissa could stay at home for the time being?' He reached into his jacket pocket and tossed their passports onto the coffee table. 'We aren't thinking of absconding.'

Baxter gave them a reassuring look. 'I think we can arrange that,' he said. 'We'll come by sometime tomorrow afternoon to get signed statements from each of you, and that should suffice for the time being. Just one further question, Mrs Littlewood. When was the last time you saw Mrs Evans and put a tablet in her tea?'

'That would have been Thursday of last week,' Melissa replied. She looked at the floor and added, 'I gave her two tablets then.'

Baxter cast a fleeting glance in her husband's direction but saw that he was looking at the floor, too. 'Well that's it for this evening. Thank you very much for assisting us with our enquiries,' he said. He stood up and wished them a good night's rest.

Out on Clifton Road Baxter grinned at Sanderson. 'Busy day tomorrow, don't you think? I'm heading for the station to file a preliminary report. You should phone Ali and Sam right now before you head home and tell them to meet us in the staff room at 8.00 am sharp for a briefing. We need a few more instances of blackmail and warfarin revenge to sort this case out.'

* * *

Akiko was asleep when Baxter finally got home, but she awoke when he slipped into bed beside her. 'Hi,' she said groggily. 'Any progress?'

'Hmm, yes,' he muttered as he switched on the alarm clock and put his arms around her. They were both fast asleep moments later.

CHAPTER 18

'Blackmail!' Akiko exclaimed over tea and toast early on Saturday morning. 'How intriguing. And you think she was extracting payments from some of her other clients, too. On the same grounds?'

'Maybe,' Baxter replied, 'or maybe she found other skeletons in their closets. Exton dons are not immune to any of the usual human frailties, and we know Mrs Evans was always interested in the latest gossip. It's likely, too, that she checked out everyone's email and other correspondence whenever she had the chance, not just Littlewood's. At any rate, I'm pretty sure Mrs Littlewood didn't give her enough warfarin to do her in, so we'll try to find out today who else might have dosed her teas or coffees. Sorry to rush you, my sweet, but I've got to be at the station by 8.00.'

They got dressed hurriedly and headed for Baxter's car.

'Not the ideal way to spend our last day together,' Baxter said as he sped down the Abingdon Road. 'I'll come back for you as soon as I can.'

'Good hunting, James,' Akiko said as he turned into the driveway of the Lodgings a few minutes later. She gave him a brief kiss on the cheek, got out of the car and waved as he drove away.

* * *

Baxter was surprised to see Susan Andrews in the staff room when he arrived at 7.55. 'Ali phoned me late last night,' she said, 'and I figured this would be a lot more interesting than cleaning my house and doing the laundry. Ali and I will join forces to interview the Thompsons and the Avery-Hills if that's okay with you. Ali's still a bit uncomfortable dealing with people with fancy degrees. Sam can stay here and record the details for any media report we're able to make later today.'

'All right,' Baxter replied, 'but do encourage Ali to ask questions, too. He's got a good nose for lies and half-truths.'

'I agree,' Susan said. 'How do you think we should treat the "new development in the case" when we start talking to these people?'

'Let's go the empathy route, say it has just come to our attention that Mrs Evans was blackmailing one of her clients, and we're concerned she may have been putting pressure of some sort on them, too,' Baxter said. 'Not a word about warfarin, but take it from there as and when we can.'

'No one finds it easy to admit to being blackmailed, James,' Susan said.

'True,' Baxter replied, 'but these people are smart enough to know we can get writs to examine their bank records if necessary. And if any of them did slip a tablet or two into Mrs Evans's hot drink or lemonade, they just might figure it's in their interest to take advantage of the mitigating factor we're dangling before them.'

* * *

'Good grief,' said Sidney Marsden, specialist in Development Studies and Senior Research Fellow of St

Edward's. 'I would never have thought Paula capable of blackmail, but that said, I have been told on more than one occasion that I'm pretty unworldly.'

'Usually by me,' his wife Carolyn added with a smile. 'I don't suppose you can give us any details?'

'Not at this time, I'm afraid,' Baxter replied. 'Did you like Mrs Evans, Mrs Mardsen?'

'I only met her once, a year or so ago when Sid was recovering from his by-pass surgery,' Mrs Marsden answered. 'She brought some of his post by the house just as I was dashing off to teach my yoga class. She was in a hurry, too, so we didn't have time to chat.'

'As I told your inspector, I almost always saw Paula in college,' her husband added. 'Except when I was recuperating for a month or so here at home.'

'And your health is much improved now, I trust,' Baxter said.

'Oh yes,' Marsden said. 'A new lease on life, just as the consultant promised. I've lost most of the excess weight I was carrying around and now only take the usual pills to keep my cholesterol and blood pressure down. Carolyn says I'm even getting better at yoga.'

'Well I'm glad to hear that,' Baxter said, 'and thank you for seeing us. We'll be on our way now.'

'One down, one to go,' he said as he and Sanderson got back into his car. 'There's no warfarin in that household, I figure, so we can strike the Marsdens from our list, at least for the time being.'

Susan phoned Sanderson just as Baxter was parking on Angel's Lane in South Exton, and Sanderson put the phone in high-volume mode so Baxter could hear what she said.

'Ali and I agree that the Thompsons seemed genuinely shocked at our news,' she reported, 'and thoroughly bemused by our concerns for them. Mrs Thompson was particularly scandalized that anyone of "our sort", as she put it, would commit a misdeed, and second, cave in to a blackmail attempt. Apparently, they're both crime fiction buffs – probably the only redeeming feature they have – and they ended up having quite a spirited debate about how much prison time most of the blackmail victims in the genre would have had to spend if they'd just gone to the police and confessed, as compared to the risk of their ending up dead at some point in the novels concerned. She's something of a mathematician, too, it seems, and they started quoting theorems and odds that lost me from the outset. Ali hung in there longer and even cited a novel focused on blackmail that neither of them had read. He's promised to loan them his copy if they can't find it elsewhere. Anyway, we're on our way back to the station now since we don't see the Avery-Hills until noon. Your news?'

'I'm thinking of taking up yoga to improve my heart health,' Baxter replied, 'but the Marsdens are otherwise out of the frame. We'll be on the Blacks' doorstep in moments. We won't be back at the station before noon, so let's keep in touch by phone.'

* * *

Steven Black, Professor of Chemistry and Fellow of Wakefield, looked decidedly haggard when he opened his front door. 'Excuse the mess,' he said as he led them to the dining room. 'My wife has been away for a couple of weeks, looking after her mother. This is the only halfway tidy room left in the house. Do sit down.'

Baxter had noted that Black had been drinking and decided to be particularly empathetic as he described the new development in the case.

'So I wasn't the only one,' Black said with just the hint of surprise in his voice.

'Why was Mrs Evans blackmailing you?' Baxter asked.

'It's a long story, and I'm not sure I can take you through it coherently,' Black answered. 'We'd taken such care to avoid emails, and most of our contacts were by our home phones or in person at conferences. But there was the occasional fax, and I guess she found enough of them in my workroom to figure it out.'

'What exactly did she figure out?' Baxter prompted.

'That I'd organized a very effective MCR network. That's short for Mutual Citing and Refereeing,' Black said. 'We didn't call it that, of course. It was known as Prochem 21, and it was practically global in scope and randomized enough to escape detection. None of this former students citing their mentors or immediate colleagues citing each other's stuff that some people went in for back in the 90s. We went well beyond that. Everyone who signed on after careful vetting had a different quota of citations to make annually and agreed to give the strongest possible support to any grant proposals they received from any source for research funding proposals submitted by another member of the network. It worked very well for everyone concerned, no matter where they were. Until Paula threatened to expose it.'

'And then you started paying her to keep quiet?' Baxter asked.

'For about a year, £100 a month in cash on top of what I owed her for secretarial work,' Black said. 'But she upped the ante to more than I was willing or able to pay last month. Said she wanted an extra payment of £2,000 for her "trip of a lifetime".' He took a deep breath and added, 'That's when I started putting a warfarin tablet or two in her tea whenever she stopped by to deliver the work she'd done for me and ask when she could expect the "extra", as she put it. I have to say it's a relief to tell you that. I didn't think the tablets would kill her, just make her ill enough to give up the idea of a round-the-world holiday, so I was startled by the piece in the *Exton Times* the other day. I'll try to sober up before I appear in court.'

'We appreciate your candour, Professor,' Baxter said. 'DC Sanderson here will help you to the car. As you're alone here, I think it best that you come with us, and we'll get you the help you need.'

'Thanks,' said Black as he rose unsteadily to his feet. 'I'm not doing at all well on my own, am I? Still, I'm glad Sandra isn't here to witness the destruction of my career.'

'This way, Professor,' Sanderson said as he guided Black to the front door and down the steps. Baxter found the house keys on a hook in the entry hall and checked that the back door was locked and all the ground floor windows were closed before locking the front door and returning to his car.

* * *

After signing Black into the secure unit at the Wallingford Hospital, Baxter and Sanderson headed back to Abingdon. They were having lunch in the staff canteen when Susan phoned at 12.30.

'We're having some trouble here, James. The Professor went ashen when I mentioned our concern for him, and his wife went ballistic. He just sat there while she launched into this tirade about "my totally outrageous suggestion" that her husband, "a world-famous scholar", could be vulnerable to blackmail of any sort. When Ali tried to calm her down by saying that we were simply checking with them to make sure everything was all right, she turned on him and told him they didn't need any help from "foreigners" like him. Then she stormed off into the garden, and Avery-Hill slumped in his chair. I've phoned for the paramedics and am sitting here holding his hand. Ali went outside to block their garage with my car just in case his missus decides to storm off onto the public highway.'

'I'll be there in fifteen minutes,' Baxter said. 'Looks like we've got another one, or possibly two,' he said to Sanderson as he stood up. 'You stay here and make a start on the statement forms. We'll probably need at least four of them, maybe five. Try your hand at a press release, too. Silvia might be impressed enough by your efforts to finally agree to go out on a date with you.' He had turned from the table and headed for the car park before Sanderson's face flushed bright red.

The arrival first of a paramedic on a motorcycle and then of an ambulance with siren sounding had drawn a few of the Avery-Hills' neighbours out of their houses and onto the pavement, but Sergeant Hussein ushered them aside to allow Baxter to park behind Susan's car in the driveway. 'Listen everyone,' Baxter heard Ali saying as he got out of his car. 'We appreciate your concern, but please go home now and allow the emergency services to do their job. You, too, kids. Why not watch the action from over there, across the street.

Much better camera angles for you when the ambulance takes off. Right now, off you go.'

Baxter headed straight for the living room and then for the garden, after Susan gave him a thumb's up to indicate that the situation there was under control. He found Daphne Avery-Hill seated on a bench by the pond.

'We meet again, Mrs Avery-Hill,' he said.

She looked up at him, a slightly dazed expression in her eyes. 'Oh yes,' she said, 'I remember you well, Inspector. Do join me on this bench. It's the best view in my garden.'

'You are very protective of your husband,' Baxter said as he sat down beside her.

'Winston needs so much protection,' she sighed. 'So much nurturing. I have encouraged him in many ways over the years, you know, and I did think he was finally poised to get a knighthood at long last. Until that woman interfered.'

'I expect you are referring to Paula Evans,' Baxter said. 'I must say I share some of your objections to her.'

'Do you now!' Daphne replied, taking his hand in hers. 'Well, let me tell you something really nasty about her. She came here a week ago yesterday, when poor Winston was just back from hospital. I wouldn't let her see him, of course, as he needed his rest, but I said I would convey any message she had for him. Then she handed me this file folder full of email print-outs, making it clear that they were copies. They were letters of reference for some sort of fellowship at TH over the past few years. She muttered something in that common way of hers about how they had been "doctored" before going to the committee, and she asked me to let Winston see them as soon as possible. "Tell him I'm prepared to keep quiet about all this," she added, and I reluctantly agreed she could come by again late Sunday morning.'

'And then?' Baxter prompted.

'Well, I read the letters straight away, of course, two versions of each one. She had highlighted the slightly different text in that ghastly yellow ink some people use, and I could see that the differences might be subject to misinterpretation,' Daphne replied. 'And all the letters were addressed to Winston! I didn't give him the folder as I didn't want to upset him unnecessarily.'

'So what did you do?' Baxter asked.

Daphne gazed at the pond and the lush planting beyond it. 'I decided we needed to be rid of Paula Evans,' she said after a pause, 'just the way I get rid of ugly weeds in my beautiful garden. I slipped three of Winston's warfarin tablets into her coffee when she came by on Sunday. She and Winston spent some time on their own in his study, and I expect she was rather mystified by his vague responses to her questions. She did give me an angry look as she left. "I'll be back," she said, and then she got on her bike and went away. Fortunately, she was not able to come back and trouble us again.'

Baxter nodded and invited Daphne to come with him. He held on to her hand as they returned to the house and then into his car.

CHAPTER 19

'Such lovely roses,' said Elizabeth as she sipped tea from a fine china cup in the Warden's garden late on Saturday afternoon. 'It's so peaceful here.'

Just then Baxter's car turned into the driveway and came to a screeching halt.

'Please excuse me,' said Akiko as she got up and ran across the lawn.

'It's the police again,' said Tom. 'There's been a murder, you see.'

'Our Japanese visitor and the DCI in charge of the case have fallen madly in love,' added Sir Christopher.

'Good gracious!' said Elizabeth. 'I had no idea there was such drama in Exton colleges. Except on television, of course.'

A few moments later Baxter and Akiko came around the corner of the house arm in arm, all smiles.

'Good news?' asked Sir Christopher.

'Yes, sir!' said Baxter. 'I think we've got it nailed. We have three confessions, one from a professor and two from other professors' wives. It all adds up. Your Professor Avery-Hill's wife was the last one to crack.'

'I thought you said "a murder", Tom,' Elizabeth exclaimed. 'This sounds more like mass murder to me.'

Sir Christopher hurriedly introduced her to Baxter and

then turned to Tom. 'Perhaps you might take Elizabeth on a tour of the grounds,' he said.

'Thank you for your concern, Sir Christopher,' said Elizabeth, 'but I'm staying here. My late husband was a QC for decades and I'm sure I've heard worse. This sounds quite fascinating, in fact. Do tell us more, Inspector.'

Baxter sat down, and Akiko sat down beside him. 'There's just one corpse, Mrs Adams,' he said, 'and no murder. Well, you could call it an unplanned collective murder, I suppose, but we're treating it as three separate instances of grievous bodily harm, GBH, against one person.' He gave an account of recent events and then turned to Sir Christopher. 'Your Professor Avery-Hill is mightily upset. He says his career has been ruined by the one person he trusted most in the world. No mention of his own misdeeds that were the source of it all, of course. He muttered something about making a fresh start somewhere far away or maybe just packing it all in.'

'I will certainly prompt Winston in those directions,' said Sir Christopher. 'Right then, you two should head off and enjoy yourselves, and I must give the Bursar a call. We need to get ready for the inevitable enquiries from the press and draft an e-mail to the fellowship. Elizabeth, I do hope you will visit us again on a slightly less dramatic day. I regret that I must now hand you over to Tom, but I'm sure he will give you an excellent guided tour of TH.'

'What sort of penalties do you think the Crown Prosecutors will go for,' asked Elizabeth as she shook Baxter's hand.

'There are extenuating circumstances, as you will be aware,' Baxter replied, 'Most of all, the actual or attempted blackmail these people experienced. With the right barristers, maybe three or four years? Maybe less. Maybe the juries will decide that public knowledge of the actions that made them vulnerable to blackmail is punishment enough. Some sort of justice will be done.'

'And goodbye to you, my dear,' Elizabeth said to Akiko. 'My brother is so delighted with all the advice you've given him. Do have a pleasant evening with this exceedingly attractive DCI you've found.' She then took Tom's arm, and they headed off toward the main quad.

Sir Christopher gave Baxter an avuncular pat on the shoulder, Akiko a kiss on her cheek and headed to the Lodgings.

'So where to?' asked Akiko.

'Let's go home,' Baxter said, putting his arm around her and heading across the lawn. 'We can order in a pizza for an early supper and have some more of those interesting strawberries for dessert. I'm off duty until Monday, and I've given Sanderson strict instructions not to disturb me unless civil insurrection has broken out.'

CHAPTER 20

Sir Christopher and the Bursar ended their message to the fellowship with an invitation to an informal gathering at the Lodgings at 8.30 that evening, and most of the fellows who were still in Exton turned up. Winston Avery-Hill's name had, of course, been deleted from the mailing list.

Tom had set up a bar on the dining room table and made a large urn of coffee. People clustered in small groups, talking quietly. Sir Christopher moved from group to group, answering questions. Finally he cleared his throat and spoke to the gathering as a whole.

'Thank you all for coming this evening,' he said. 'We've had some shocking news today, and I'm as startled and upset by it as the rest of you. It's good to have a chance to get together as colleagues and share our concerns. And we need to brace ourselves for the media spotlight that will hit TH tomorrow.'

'The usual drill?' asked Elliot Jameson.

'Yes,' Sir Christopher replied. 'Decline to give interviews and refer anyone who contacts you to our Public Relations Officer. David and I have drafted a statement, and she'll fax them copies of it. The statement focuses on the sad death of Paula Evans, a part-time college employee, and says we understand that the Thames Valley Police have made several arrests. We have helped the police with their enquiries and remain willing to do so. No names are mentioned, but it won't be long before we get asked about Winston. I'm prepared to acknowledge that his wife is one of those arrested, and we feel deeply concerned about him at what must be a very difficult time. No further details.'

'So Winston is going to get out of this unscathed?' asked Ray Chang.

'I rather expect Winston will be submitting his resignation soon,' Sir Christopher replied. 'I'll mention that we are aware of the records Bates kept when I drop by to see him tomorrow. Once he's read Daphne's statement and those doctored references that Mrs Evans delivered to her, he'll know he doesn't stand a chance in any disciplinary proceedings we undertake. And I suspect the media will soon get hold of enough of the facts in all three cases of blackmail or attempted blackmail to do very serious damage to the reputations of those concerned. Winston is going to suffer, as well he should, but it will be easier for us if he simply resigns and disappears.'

'It's not going to be easier for us with HEFCE,' muttered Owen Magnusson. 'Steve Black's sophisticated citation game is going to offend them deeply, and they'll come up with even more complicated ways to measure the impact of our publications.'

'Ah yes, even more complicated measurement,' said Sidney Ashwood, Professor of Ethics, with a sigh. 'But it's the attempt at measurement itself that is the root of the problem. If I cite someone's flawed argument in one of my publications, that counts as much in his or her favour as a positive evaluation! Quantity of citations is simply no indicator of quality, just as being talked about a lot is no indicator of one's merit.'

Jason Brown, Lecturer in Biochemistry, chuckled. 'That's

precisely the case with the paper that topping the citations list in my field at the moment. It contained a serious error in methodology, so practically everyone has had a go at it. With the result that its author looks like a superstar to the number crunchers in his university.'

Professor Ashwood sighed again. 'There must be some way we can extricate ourselves from this morass. Not just the mindless quantification. All this pressure for immediate "relevance" and "utility" to the world beyond academe is stifling serious thinking *within* universities. And if we academics don't think seriously about our subjects we can't teach our students well. Research and teaching used to be seen as interdependent, but that link has been broken by successive governments. Higher education is no longer deemed a public good in and of itself. It is merely another means to individual and collective profit.'

Elliot Jameson spoke up from the far side of the room. 'There's no going back to the "good old days", Sid, not without a sea change in the thinking of our political masters, and that's unlikely. Greater autonomy from the state might help. It's no coincidence that most of the leading universities in the USA are private institutions with their own endowments. Exton and a few other universities here might be able to take that route eventually, but getting contributions without strings attached – posts in trendy, new fields, new projects of particular interest to benefactors – will be a challenge. And HEFCE and the research councils will still be able to call the shots when it comes to funding for big research projects.'

'So we're stuck in the morass?' asked Adele Williamson. 'Is there nothing we can do?'

'We can publicize our concerns, I suppose,' Jameson said.

'A few more critiques of state policy in the newspapers, a few more defences of curiosity-driven research might help. We academics have been remarkably passive about all these changes, you know. We've grumbled, but basically we've done what we've been told to do.'

'What about the appraisal scheme here at Exton?' Ray Chang asked. 'That's coming up for a vote in the Academic Assembly in November. Unlike at most universities in this country we academics here do still have some sort of say in what happens. But do we have any chance of defeating the proposal?'

'I'm certainly voting against it,' said Professor Ashwood. 'A good book should count for more than an article. And research should remain as independent as possible from government and its short-term concerns.'

'What about all the emphasis on media exposure!' Adele Williamson exclaimed. 'That's fine for those whose research coincides with the top news stories of the day, but who's going to be interested in my work on family planning in Central America? It's only when there's a natural disaster or a coup in the region that someone from the media contacts me for the background information on the country that they just as easily could have got from a good world almanac or even more quickly from Wikipedia.'

'The proposal assumes there will be losers as well as winners,' added Jason Brown. 'But what if the majority of us get high scores? Will the University reward us all, or will they cook the figures to ensure a spread that fits the payroll budget? HEFCE changes the payout rules whenever too many units of assessment within universities score too highly, so I wouldn't put it past our management tier to do the same.'

'And who is going to conduct those "career development" interviews with the people who get low scores?' asked Ray Chang. 'Someone with a Masters in personnel management, I suspect, who has never published an article, much less a book. I bet they'll get bonuses for every low-scoring academic they browbeat into getting a post at a more "suitable" institution.'

Jameson was beaming. 'Well,' he said, 'you have certainly identified a number of problems with the proposal. I wouldn't be surprised if many of our colleagues in other colleges have similar misgivings. But grumbling among ourselves again won't do. We need to mobilize.'

'I could invite some of the proposal's drafters to a Q&A session here next week,' said the Bursar. 'I'd remind them that we didn't receive the proposal until late May, just as the exam season was starting, and say we'd like clarification of a few points now that we've had time to consider what they've put forward.'

'An excellent idea, David,' said Sir Christopher. 'I'll phone the other Heads of House and suggest they do the same. We've been accounting for ourselves to management for years. It's high time management had to account for itself.'

'We could draft a paper after the session, outlining our reservations,' said Professor Ashwood. 'Then present it to our first Governing Body meeting in October and forward the agreed text to the Vice-Chancellor.'

'The more colleges that do the same, the better,' said Jameson. 'But we need to reach out to individual academics as well. Write some articles for the first issue of the staff magazine after the summer vacation. Maybe get up a petition telling management to go back to the drawing boards and come up with a proposal that truly rewards merit. Get the national media interested in what we're up to.'

'And line up some effective speakers for that meeting of Assembly in November,' said Sir Christopher, rubbing his hands. 'This has turned out to be a very productive evening, colleagues. Who would have thought it just a few hours ago!'

CHAPTER 21

Sunday morning a little after 9.00. Baxter and Akiko once again sat in his car in the driveway of the Lodgings.

'Well, this is it for us, for now,' Baxter said.

'Yes,' Akiko replied softly.

'And you really want to take that t-shirt of mine back with you to Tokyo?'

'I really do,' she said. 'I am incorrigibly sentimental. Besides, I need something appropriate to wear when we're bumping into each other in my tiny kitchen in Naka-Meguro.'

Baxter smiled and stroked her cheek. 'I wish I could take you to Heathrow, but I've got to get to Sheffield by lunchtime.'

'I understand completely,' Akiko replied. 'Besides, it will be fun driving to the airport with Tom. You and I would just get more and more miserable with every passing mile, and then I'd have Sophie's tears at missing her grandpa on her birthday on my conscience. You're going to have a wonderful day, James. We'll have our own wonderful days again soon.'

'You bet we will,' Baxter said. 'Come on then, the least I can do is to see you properly to the door for once.' They got out of the car and walked hand in hand to the steps.

'I am so glad I met you, James,' Akiko said as she stood on tiptoe to kiss him.

Baxter put his arms around her and held her close. 'Have

a good flight,' he whispered in her ear. 'Don't go an inch farther than Tokyo.'

Akiko smiled up at him. 'Not a millimetre,' she murmured.

He kissed her lightly on her nose, watched her go inside and headed back to his car.

* * *

Sir Christopher rose from his chair in the living room when he heard the front door close. 'Ah, there you are,' he said. 'Everything okay?'

'Yes, Warden,' Akiko replied. 'I hope you haven't been sitting there worrying about me for long.'

'Well, maybe I was worrying just a bit,' Sir Christopher said apologetically. 'But come, I've really been lying in wait for you because I have something to show you.' He led her to the library, where Tom's watercolour of Lucy now rested on the mantelpiece. 'Isn't it lovely,' he said. 'It's brought so many memories back, and reminded me of some of the things about her, like that dimple there on her left cheek, that I had forgotten. I thought the portrait should be in the living room, over by the piano, but Tom insisted it belonged here. I have a sneaking suspicion Elizabeth conspired with him about that yesterday afternoon. We'll get it framed, of course.'

'Tom's right,' said Akiko, wiping away tears with Baxter's t-shirt. 'The scale of this room is just perfect, and so is the dimmer lighting. It truly is a lovely portrait.'

'There, there, Akiko,' Sir Christopher said as he hugged her. 'I know it's tough for you this morning. I hate seeing you unhappy, especially when I'm so happy. You've mended much more than a vase while you've been here with us!'

'I'm just the slightest bit wobbly,' Akiko murmured as she relaxed into the Warden's comforting arms, 'but I'm not unhappy. Not really. There's so much to look forward to.'

'Indeed there is,' Sir Christopher said warmly. 'The fellows of TH may even have made a start on freeing themselves and their colleagues from mindless metrics! Now, how about a cup of coffee? Tom says you don't have to head off to Heathrow until 10.00.'

'Yes, please,' said Akiko brightly. They headed for the kitchen. 'Aren't you worried about Tom and Elizabeth conspiring together?' she asked.

'Not in the least, my dear,' Sir Christopher replied. 'As you so cogently observed just the other day, my son and I are quite a double act.'